ALSO BY CHRIS LYNCH

This Book Belongs To
Mrs. Langdon

INEXCUSABLE

chris lynch

Simon Pulse
New York · London · Toronto · Sydney

SIMON PULSE

An imprint of Simon & Schuster Children's Publishing Division
1230 Avenue of the Americas, New York, NY 10020
Copyright © 2005 by Chris Lynch
All rights reserved, including the right of reproduction
in whole or in part in any form.
SIMON PULSE and colophon are registered trademarks of Simon & Schuster, Inc.
Also available in an Atheneum hardcover edition.
Designed by Kristin Smith and Jessica Sonkin
The text of this book was set in Proforma.
Manufactured in the United States of America
First Simon Pulse edition May 2007
2 4 6 8 10 9 7 5 3 1
The Library of Congress has cataloged the hardcover edition as follows:
Lynch, Chris.
Inexcusable / Chris Lynch.—1st ed.
p. cm.
"Ginnee Seo Books."
Summary: High school senior and football player Keir sets out to enjoy
himself on graduation night, but when he attempts to comfort a friend
whose date has left her stranded, things go terribly wrong.
ISBN-13: 978-0-689-84789-9 (hc)
ISBN-10: 0-689-84789-0 (hc)
[1. Rape—Fiction. 2. High schools—Fiction. 3. Schools—Fiction.
4. Family life—Fiction. 5. Alcohol—Fiction. 6. Football—Fiction.] I. Title.
PZ7.9845Way 2005
[Fic]—dc22
2004030874
ISBN-13: 978-1-4169-3972-6 (pbk)
ISBN-10: 1-4169-3972-5 (pbk)

INEXCUSABLE

T he way it looks is not the way it is.

Gigi Boudakian is screaming at me so fearsomely, I think I could just about cry. I almost don't even care what the subject is because right now I am sick and I am confused and I am laid so low by the very idea that Gigi Boudakian is screaming at me that the what-for hardly seems even to matter. I love Gigi Boudakian. I hate it when people I love scream at me.

And I don't feel guilty. That is, I don't feel like I *am* guilty. But I sure as hell feel sorry.

I am sorry.

I am one sorry sorry bastard. And I feel very sick.

I am so sorry.

"What are you sorry for, Keir?" Gigi screams again, grabbing me by where my lapels would be if I had a jacket on, or a shirt, or anything. She can't get a purchase because I have no clothes, and very little fat, because I have been good about my health lately. She grabs, can't grab, scratches instead at my chest, then slaps me hard across the face, first right side then left, smack, smack.

"Say what you did, Keir."

"Why is Carl coming? Why do you have to call Carl, Gigi?"

"Say what you did, Keir. Admit what you did to me."

"I didn't do anything, Gigi."

"Yes you did! I said *no*!"

I say this very quietly, but firmly. "You did not."

"I said *no*," she growls. "Say it."

"I don't see why you need Carl. You can beat me up just fine on your own. Listen, Gigi, it was nobody's fault."

"Yes it was! It was *your* fault. This should not have happened."

"Fine, then it didn't."

"It did, it did, it did, bastard! For me it did, and it's making me sick."

"Don't. Don't be sick. I don't want you to be sick or anything. I just want everything to be all right. Everything is all right, Gigi. Please, can everything be all right?"

"It is not all right! It is not all right, and you are not all right, Keir Sarafian. Nothing is all right. Nothing will ever again ever be all right."

She is wrong. Gigi is wrong about everything, but

especially about me. You could ask pretty much anybody and they will tell you. *Rock solid, Keir. Kind of guy you want behind you. Keir Sarafian, straight shooter. Loyal, polite. Funny. Good manners. He was brought up right, that boy was,* is what you would hear. All the things you would want to hear said about you are the things I have always heard said about me. I am a good guy.

Good guys don't do bad things. Good guys understand that no means no, and so I could not have done this because I understand, and I love Gigi Boudakian.

"I love you, Gigi."

As I say this, Gigi Boudakian lets out the most horrific scream I have ever heard, and I am terrified by it and reach out, lunge toward her and try and cover her mouth with my hands and I fall over her and she screams louder and bites at my hands and I keep flailing, trying to stop that sound coming out of her and getting out into the world.

I am only trying to stop the sound. It looks terrible what I am doing, as I watch my hands doing it, as I watch hysterical Gigi Boudakian reacting to me, and it looks really, really terrible but I am only trying to stop the awful sound and the way it looks is not the way it is.

The way it looks is *not* the way it is.

There are verifiable reasons for the wrongness of this situation. I have character witnesses. Because I have character. I have two brainy, insightful older sisters, Mary and Fran, who brook no nonsense off anybody, and Mary and Fran love me to pieces and respect me, and they would not do that if I were capable of being monstrous. People like that don't support monsters. But they support me, Mary and Fran do. Meeting Mary and Fran would convince you I am what I say I am.

And here's another reason. If I'm going to tell you the truth, and that is exactly what I am going to do, then I would have to tell you this about me: Most of the time, I would rather go to my room and whack myself silly to a good song than to have a whole team of actual lap dancers all to myself in person. Really, truly, I would rather. Does that sound like a menace to society to you?

Really, I'm the kind of guy who would rather stay at home on a Saturday night to play a board game with his dad than go to a party. I have done that, a lot of times. Truly. Does that sound like a monster to you?

Ray never screamed at me, which was one of the many things that made him a great father, a great man. I hate it when people I love scream at me. There is no more piercing sound, there is nothing that runs you right all the way through, like having somebody you love scream at you.

What he did do was play Risk with me. My dad and I had a game of Risk going forever. It started on the Sunday night when we got back from trucking the girls off all the way to college, three hours and one state line one way and three more and one more back this way, and we came back wrecked and empty to a house without the girls in it and even though that should have come as no surprise, inside, it was a big surprise. I thought I knew, but I didn't really know, what a house without girls was going to feel like.

We stood in the doorway, looking around in the darkness, looking around as if we saw a strange car in the driveway or heard a burglar alarm wheening, and we were standing and staring and listening for what was there that shouldn't have been.

He was as tired as I was, I knew it. It was time for bed for both of us.

"I don't want to go to bed yet," he said, flipping on a light but still looking all over like everything was spooky strangeness.

"Na, I'm not ready yet either," I said.

And so the war began. It started with my Venezuela kicking squat out of his Peru, continued through my fierce razing of the rest of South America, two frozen pizzas, one tub of microwave popcorn, and half a white chocolate cheesecake.

Before we finally went to bed, I had been driven all the way back up into Canada, and pretty deep into the second half of the cheesecake.

We left the board right there, on our square maple-top dining room table that had no leaves for extensions but was always the right size for the four of us, me and Dad and Mary and Fran, for all those years, and for me and Dad and Fran since the year before when Mary left for school, and would surely be enough for just the two of us now, but not with the whole of the Risk map spread out across it. We said we'd finish up the next day, and clear the table again and eat dinner there like always, once the game was finished, and we went up to bed.

"I'm looking forward to it," he said, near the end of our bachelor year. When it was just the two of us in the house. "I can't wait for you to be gone."

Right.

"Right. Why is that, Ray?"

"Because I'm going to need all this space. Going to need all the rooms, to start my new family. To start my new, beautiful family to replace the one that left me. My brand-new, loyal family that won't leave me."

"Guilty family, you mean."

"Loyal."

"It's the same thing, probably."

He didn't mean it. Some of it, he did. He missed the girls terribly. And it was going to be worse next year when I went to school.

But I kind of doubted he was going to replace us.

"I'm going to join one of those dating services. Meet the right woman. Start making babies left and right."

"Dad, jeez," I said.

"See, you're jealous. My new family is going to be better."

Mercifully, the phone rang. Fran. She called me every day from school. Good ol' Fran. Thank god, some days, for good ol' Fran on the phone.

"So who wants to hear about his fantasy family?" she said.

"Exactly," I said. "That's what I told him. Here, let me put him on—"

"Don't you *dare*," she said.

"He'll listen to you, Fran."

"Like hell he will. He'll just get worse."

She was probably right. Nobody could really do much with Ray once he got going, once he got to having a good time. If he thought he was getting a rise out of you, he'd just keep upping the ante.

"Mary," we both said into the phone at the same time.

We said this because he'd listen to Mary. Everyone listened to Mary. There would have to be something seriously wrong with a person not to listen to Mary.

Mary was my older twin sister. Right, no. Not my twin. Well, not Fran's twin, either. They are Irish twins, y'know, born ten months apart, with Fran coming just a year ahead of me. Ray said that was just a helluva time, baby-machining, him and my mom, getting started on a complete zoo of a house full of us that they weren't ever going to stop making until somebody passed a law or something.

Or something. Or something like my mom dying, which is what she did to us.

Three years married, three kids, and bang, gone, so long, Mom.

We have a piano in this house that exists solely for the purpose of supporting her photograph.

He marches us to her spot in the cemetery about six times a year.

I didn't even know her. I wouldn't even ever have known her. Wouldn't have missed her, I don't think. If it weren't for him.

Ray loves her like she was standing right in front of him.

"You telling people about my new better family?" he said as he passed by the phone.

"Don't tell him it's me," Fran said.

"Want to talk to Fran, Dad?" I said.

"Jerk," she said.

"Franny, my Franny," Ray said, pawing at the phone like a bear at a honey pot.

Anyway, they are not twins exactly, but they look enough like twins, and they act enough like twins—in that under-each-other's-skin kind of way—that they are mostly considered to be twins.

"When are you coming home?" Ray said, sounding all wounded and needy as if he had been abandoned by the world. "And where's Mary? I want to talk to Mary."

He had no business acting abandoned. He had not been abandoned, yet.

Mary was a sophomore at the university. Fran was a freshman.

Me, I was a senior in high school, for a couple more weeks. Then in the fall I'd join the girls, if all went according to plan.

"But you'll be here for the graduation, right? You wouldn't dare miss—"

He was cut short and started nodding as I watched him there, squeezed into the too-small telephone table/chair setup. We could assume Mary had come on the phone.

He nodded more emphatically.

"She can't hear that, Dad," I said.

He waved me away, but resumed oral communication.

"Of course. Of course. Sure I know that. Sure I do."

I watched him. He was one outstanding old geezer. A geezer and a half.

He was a full-time, long-time, professional widower. There's a word for you. Widower. With that *er* at the end, making it sound like an action verb. He widowed pretty well.

And he was a pretty fine roommate, a great player of games, a sport, and a loyal best, best friend.

You had to be a good guy if you were Ray Sarafian's kid. You couldn't possibly be anything less.

I can show you how things can go wrong, how they did go wrong one other time. I can show you by showing you another thing I didn't do. Anyway, a thing I didn't do in the way some people tried to picture that I did it.

I was unfairly famous one time, for a little while. No, I was infamous. No, *notorious*.

Famous, then infamous, then notorious.

Then it all went away and things quieted back down and that's when the stuff really started happening.

But the thing is, it was all wrong. It was all unfair and incorrect and ass-backwards. None of it happened the way it should have.

Here's why I got famous. I got famous because I crippled a guy. No, that's not right. I didn't cripple a guy. He got crippled, and I was part of it. The difference is very important.

He wasn't even crippled, exactly, but he surely doesn't play football anymore.

I shouldn't even have been there. That's the thing, understand. I shouldn't even have been in that spot, in that game, that day. I don't normally play cornerback, see. I am second-string cornerback. Mostly I'm a kicker. I'm first-string kicker, third-string tight end, and second-string cornerback.

This is significant because of the league we played in. This was not a passing league. This was not a razzle-dazzle league where the ball and the buzz were in the air all the time and there were scouts here from big-time motion-offense colleges like Miami and Southern Cal looking for talent. This was just another lopey suburban league like a million other suburban leagues around the country, full of white wide receivers and built around fullbacks who got their jobs based on the fact that their backs were very full indeed, like the view of a grand piano from above.

So the passing game was not an important thing. Not important to the game, and surely not important to me. Understand, I could have been a starter for this team, as a cornerback or as a tight end. Coach wanted me, in fact, always badgered me, to play more. But I didn't want to play more. I wanted to play less. Because I was wasting my life at cornerback and tight end. Because I wasn't good. Good enough for this team? Sure. Good enough for any decent college in America?

I had a better chance of ice dancing in the Olympics.

Kicker, though, was a different story. There was a reasonable chance I could slip in as a placekicker on a respectable small-to-midsize program if I worked hard at it.

So I did. And every year I played a little less offense and defense where I might get mangled, and spent a lot more time on the sidelines kicking the air out of that ball, out of the hands of whoever would hold for me, into that practice net over and over and over.

Until Coach dragged me into the game. Other guys needed a breather here and there. And I was no liability on the field, so I had to do my bit when called upon.

Matter of fact, I was an improvement on the guys I replaced. Because I always did what I was told. I always did it by the numbers. I always followed the plan. And I always gave it full tilt.

That is me. If I am any good at anything it is because I do it just like that. Do like you're taught, do it by the numbers, and do it maximum, and you will do something well. I figure.

I wasn't looking for any full-time cornerback job, and I wasn't looking to catch the eye of some Division III scout looking for defensive backs. I was looking to get the job done the way I was taught, and get back to the sidelines where I could kick and kick and remain safe, and get the easiest possible college scholarship so that my dad could come and see me at Homecoming and not have to remortgage the house to pay for the privilege. My dad could come on some excellent Homecoming day, my sisters would be up there, Mary on his right and Fran on his left, sitting up there in the sharp freezing November sun and then they would be able to see me run onto the field at the end of a big game and *bang* that ball through the posts, just as cool as you like.

That would be the moment, wouldn't it? That would be the best. Every eye on me, because the kicker is the only one who can do that, hold every eye, hold the game close to himself, and then Fran and Mary and Dad would be on their feet, screaming louder than everyone, so proud they could just expire, and I would wave dramatically at them, and later we would go to a nice restaurant and I would eat like a king and listen to the best people I knew telling me I was very good.

That was my dream. That was as far as my dream went, and I would have stacked my dream up against anyone's.

Which is why I shouldn't have been on the field that day. I should have been working on my field goals, because guys were starting to get their offer letters from schools and I wasn't. I had had some interest from schools, but you would have to call it tepid if you called it anything.

Understand. I should not have been on that field. They should not have had me on that field. I had to kick if I was going to get anywhere.

But first, there was business. It was late in the season,

in a game that didn't matter to the state championships or the league standings or even to any of the parents of the players beyond the twelve or so in the stands, but for some reason, the quarterback on the other team started going mental. One of those parents had to be his, and he must have been aware that one or more of the others was a scout with a desperate need for a quarterback and an offer letter in his fist, and that quarterback must have been opening his mail every morning just like I was, to the same screaming lack of interest from the college football fraternity with time whipping by at whiplash speed.

Because he started to throw. The sonofabitch started to throw. And throw and throw and throw.

I even had to stop kicking to watch. He was immense. He was a monster. I was thinking, jeez, if you had just thrown like this the last three years you could be sitting at home right now comparing illegal incentives from Nebraska and LSU instead of busting your hump trying to get somebody's attention now.

But he sure was kicking snot out of us. All our defensive players—from our tubbo linemen to our confused concrete linebackers to our backs who circled and flailed their arms looking like they were flagging down help for one car wreck after another—were absolutely ragged. They had their tongues dragging on the ground as they lamely pursued the quarterback, then when they missed him, missed the ball, then when they missed that, missed the receivers. Replacement defenders were shoved onto the field after every play.

Which is how I came to be there, when I shouldn't have been. When fate and the coach and the devil shoved me in there.

I did what I was told. I did what I was taught. I did what I did, what I always did, what I still always do. I followed things to the letter of the law. And I followed things to the spirit of the law.

It is a game played to a particularly rough spirit. It's a fact. Some would call it violent. Functioning within that specific world is not the same thing as functioning within the regular one. Circumstances change things.

They were getting away with a lot of over-the-middle stuff. Anybody could see that. It's elemental. You cannot just let a team keep throwing the ball right over the middle, behind your linebackers and in front of your corners and safeties, and not make them pay for that. Everybody understands this, and if they don't, then they need to try.

They teach you that from very early on. I learn my lessons. I comprehend the game. I play as I am taught.

Stick 'em.

I saw it unfolding again, the same way I saw it unfolding from the sidelines, play after play, when the guys on the field could probably guess what was happening but were just too whipped to do anything about it.

The quarterback took the snap, took three quick long strides back into his pocket, and let sail with a motion too quick practically to even see, more like a baseball catcher throwing out a runner.

The receiver, my guy, my responsibility, was just slanting off his pattern, angling across toward the middle of the field.

You could see it from a mile. There was no decision to be made, really. There was not more than one possible thing for me to do. There was in fact exactly one thing for me to do.

I could have closed my eyes and hit him. I mean, right from near the start of the play, I could have shut my eyes tight and still run full steam, and still arrived at just the right spot at just the right time, me, him, and the ball, because they were doing it so textbook, so simply, so thoughtlessly. It had been too easy. We had made it too easy. They were getting too comfortable. Too lazy, spoiled, entitled. You need to never do that. Never, ever, ever. It is inexcusable. It is so dangerous out there, you can never ever get spoiled, just because it is coming too easy to you. If you do that, you create a situation of your own danger, of your own making, which otherwise would not have existed, and you put me in a position to do the only thing there is to do.

When you hit a guy with all your being, hit him the way

a car hits a moose, you would expect it to hurt both of you. But it doesn't hurt the hitter, if the hitter has hit perfectly. It is a strange sensation, almost a magical sensation. The car takes a crumpling, and the moose takes a mangling.

But not the hitter. Not if you do it right, do it the way you have been taught to do it by guys who have smashed into a hundred thousand other guys before and who were taught by guys who had smashed into a hundred thousand other guys.

It's like you smash right through him. Like he's not even there. You go in, you go down, and you just find yourself there, lying as if you are just getting up out of bed. You feel nothing bad. You feel relaxed, in fact, refreshed. You even hear a short soundtrack come out of him, a kind of a grunt-cry voice forced up through fluid, through his nose, that would be scary if you heard it anywhere else. It isn't scary when you hit a guy so perfectly, though, it is something entirely else. It almost sounds like ecstasy when you play it over in your head as you get up and trot off, just a little, little bit horny.

My timing was perfect. The defensive back hit the receiver at the instant the ball arrived. A beautiful pop and explosion, like fireworks.

And that was that.

I was already on the sidelines before I knew anything. I was already back, picking up my practice ball, grabbing somebody by the jersey to come hold for me so I could kick a few and make up for lost time and get a yard closer to an offer, a college program, a Saturday game and a nice restaurant with my nice people.

I never received so many hard slaps on the back.

It wasn't a fumble, because he never had a chance to get possession of the ball. It just popped up in the air, straight up, just like the guy's helmet did, and somebody, some straggler from my team who was just standing around waiting to get lucky, got lucky, and caught the ball. Then he fell down, and a lot of other guys fell on top of him.

Great. We were on offense now, and I was off to the sidelines.

Where I became a small-time short-term hero.

"Way to bang him, Keir," somebody said, and banged me on the back.

"Way to stick."

"Mowed him, Keir. Absolutely killed him."

Until it stopped. All of it. Nobody touched me then, nobody said anything more. Some goddamn monster vacuum came and sucked all the sound, all the air and life out of the whole field, as every eye turned to the spot. The spot where I was a few seconds earlier, where I did my job as well as it can be done, where all the coaches were now and all the referees, and several people from up in the stands, and where people were looking back toward the school buildings and waving, waving for even more people to come.

I stood there, all vacuumed out myself, feeling like a head in a helmet floating above where my body should have been.

My holder walked away.

It was news. There were inquiries and investigations and editorials. I was home from school for a week, for my own good, for my peace of mind, because I couldn't possibly concentrate, couldn't hear a word with the constant roar in my ears coming from inside my own head and from all points around it. The phone rang all the time, and my dad answered it. He never put me on the phone, never shied away from a question, never lost his patience with school officials or local radio or whoever. He took off work and stayed there with me and played Risk, the game burning on all week as we took great chunks of continents from each other and then lost them again in between phone calls and lots of silence and lots of talks where he said not much more than that everything was going to work out all right and that it didn't much matter anyway what any investigation said because he already knew, knew me, and knew that his internal, in-his-own-heart investigation had cleared me.

"You're a good boy," he reminded me every time I needed reminding.

I didn't look at the mail. He did that, too. I could tell, though, if he had opened any letters from college football programs. He hadn't. No acceptances, no rejections the entire week.

No acceptances, no rejections. It was as if I did not exist. No acceptances, no rejections. That's being exactly nobody, that's what that is.

By Friday of the week I stayed home, everybody had looked into the accident. It was an accident. And also, it was no accident, anything but an accident. Everybody concluded—though not happily—that I had not done anything wrong. I had not done anything out of line. I had not done anything blameworthy.

"An unfortunately magnificent hit, in the universe of football" was what the writer called it, in the article about my being cleared.

The game, Risk, was unchanged at the end of that sorry week. It was right back where we'd started it. In stock car racing, when there is a wreck on the track, they wave the yellow flag, which means everybody keeps driving, but nobody passes anybody else, nobody changes position, they just continue, motor on, high-speed float, until things are stabilized and you can race again. We ran that week under a yellow flag, me and Dad.

Quietly, I returned to classes the following Monday. Everybody made a great effort to put the incident away, back, in the background, one tackle, late in a game, late in the season, very late in a high school football life. Very possibly the end of my football life.

When I got home, at the end of that first quiet day, I got the mail and opened it.

I had quietly received an offer of a football scholarship.

The next day I quietly received two more.

Fate is a bitch, but there you go.

Gigi Boudakian has her head in her hands, and that is all wrong. If you knew Gigi Boudakian you would agree with me that she should never have her head in her hands. She should be happy, like, every minute, because she deserves it. And for christ's sake, she should not be here with her head in her hands now, here with me, like this.

"This is all wrong, Gigi."

"You got that right, Keir," she says, still with her head in her hands, still with her eyes to the floor.

"You are my friend, Gigi, forever. I love you, Gigi."

"Shut . . . up."

"Why does Carl have to come, Gigi? I don't understand at all. And your father, and my father, and everybody. There is no reason for this. No reason. Miscommunication is all that really happened here, that's all. I thought one thing, you thought another thing. Why do you have to make it worse? Carl has been my friend forever, just like you have been my friend forever, so why do we have to make an accident into something else? I love you, Gigi."

"Shut ... up."

"You know I could never do anything to hurt you. You know I am the very last person in the world to ever do anything like that. I am a good guy and you are a smart girl, and we are us, so this could never be wrong the way you say it is. You know that! So why don't you just *know* it, and know that you don't have to say to Carl or to anybody else what you are thinking of saying?"

Finally, for the first time in a while, something in the world goes as it should go. Gigi Boudakian removes her head from her hands and looks up at me.

If she sees me, if she really sees me, everything will be all right. All right like always.

"I *thought* I knew all that, Keir. And you don't understand, that's what makes this even more horrible."

Gigi Boudakian has her head in her hands again, and it feels like nothing will ever be right ever again.

I only ever wanted to go to the one school all along, to be honest. So I was lucky. Sure there were other schools, other teams, other weekend visits to campuses, boy oh boy, were there other weekend visits.

But I never wanted to go anywhere else. I never wanted to go to fun-in-the-sun in California or Florida. I don't need the sun for fun. I can have fun in the snow, or in the mud. Or indoors. I didn't want to go to some ivy-choked four-hundred-year-old snot factory, either, even if they'd have me, which they pretty damn well certainly wouldn't. All I ever wanted was to wind up at a place about three hours and one state line from home, not closer, not farther away. A place with a reasonable sports budget, a place where a guy could have some laughs, play some ball, meet some people, and get himself educated and experienced without an excess of fuss or, especially, muss.

"You big baby," my sister Fran said, laughing when I finally told her, over the phone, of my decision to follow her and my sister Mary to Norfolk U.

"Cut it out, Fran, it had nothing to do with you guys."

"Mary," Fran was yelling away from the phone. "Mary, you have to hear this."

"Knock it off, Fran," I said.

But I didn't mind. I didn't mind at all, really. I was looking forward to it, in fact, and would, in further fact, have been disappointed if I didn't catch some grief from them for my news. There was nobody anywhere who gave me grief since they'd been gone. Everyone needs grief.

"Sure, Fran," I said, "just go ahead, go on, zoo me all you want. Just remember, I'm coming. Be forewarned. Your holiday is over once I get there."

"Oooh, I'm scared. Mary!" she screamed this practically in my ear. "Mary, Keir is being scary. You want to hear it? It's very cute."

Everybody involved was very happy to see me going to Norfolk. We were all sweating it out when I was not hearing and not hearing from the school for so many weeks, because we did all want to be together again. We're good together, us. We're good together, and less good apart, even if they sounded pretty okay. So it was a treat we were getting reunited.

Except for Dad, of course. We were getting de-united from Dad. I didn't like even thinking about that.

But he was the biggest booster of all, once the pressure was off, once the letter came through and my decision was made, no matter what circumstances might have prompted that college to send that letter to this modestly gifted athlete.

"What does Dad think?" Mary asked, now that the two of them were hogging one phone.

"Dad thinks it's the greatest," Dad said, from his sneaky bastard phone in his bedroom.

"Get off the phone, y'sneaky bastard," I shouted into the receiver while all three of them laughed at me. "Don't *make* me come in there, old man," I added when I didn't hear a click.

That was how it was, and I loved how it was, the year with Dad and me, me and Dad, father and son, brothers, roommates, bastards, and buddies in the absence of anybody else in the house. Nobody ever had it like we had it.

And with that letter, with that decision to go to Norfolk, I had to end it. To put a bullet into the beloved beast.

"You still there, Dad?" Fran said into the phone because nobody could tell if he was still listening. No breathing, no laughing, no nothing.

"Dad?" Mary asked. "We didn't really want you to hang up, silly man. Dad?"

He wasn't there. It was just the three of us now.

"Well, really, Keir," Fran said. "This is just the best news. The best."

"The best," Mary agreed. "We are very, very happy for you, Keir. Happy that it worked out, awful as it was."

"Yes, and at least there's that. It's tragic, the whole thing, that poor kid, but at least you can take something from it, that you learned a hard lesson."

A thick silence came over the line.

"A lesson, Fran?"

"Well, ya. One would certainly hope so."

The silence returned.

"I didn't learn any lesson. There was no lesson to be learned."

"Come on, Keir," Mary said. "Come on now. You dodged a bullet. Very good for you. But that doesn't mean that what happened wasn't—"

"Should I show you the newspaper, Mary? Huh? The *Chronicle* says it was an accident. It was an accident. What lesson can you learn from an accident, other than be careful? I'm being careful, Mary, if that's what you would like to hear."

"He's all yours," Mary said to Fran, with an angry little sigh.

See, the thing with Mary is she's all black and white. I mean, I love her, and she is loyal as they come, true blue. But she is rigid about right and wrong. She is a very hard person, and she can be intolerant. Fran's not like that.

"It's important that you learn, Keir. Life teaches you a lot of lessons and if you won't accept them, then it's like you've completely missed the class."

The silence again. They were getting longer, and I realized, they were all me.

"Haven't I just been through all this, Fran? Haven't I paid my dues with waiting to find out if I was responsible for what happened? Well, I waited, and I found out, and I'm not. So I'm not going to apologize when I didn't do anything wrong, and I'm not going to let you guys make me feel like hell, because I didn't do anything wrong."

"Do you think about the other kid?"

"Of course I think about the other kid."

"You don't sound like you're thinking about him that much. Did you have to hit him exactly that hard?"

"I hit him exactly the way I was taught. I hit him right. If he just stood up again I would have been a goddamn hero, wouldn't I? I did what I was supposed to do. He didn't do what he was supposed to do."

Big fat silence. Not mine this time.

I waited for it to break. I waited, and I squirmed. Fran didn't do this, you see. Fran talked. Clamming up was my move. Fran talked through whatever came.

"Fran," I finally said. "Fran, stop it, you know I can't stand that."

"I am going to assume," she said in a sticky drawly voice, like she hated to hand the words over, "that you're still hurting from what happened. That you still need to hold back from this stuff. So I'm going to leave it for now, Keir. For now."

I would have thought that I would be more than satisfied with her leaving it. I surprised myself.

"Why do I have to feel sorry if I didn't do anything wrong? I don't understand that, and I don't understand how that helps that kid at all."

"It doesn't. It helps you. And I would figure *that* was a cause you could support."

"Well, I *don't*," I snapped without thinking.

We sat there then, the two of us collaborating on a whopping great silence. It gave me a shiver.

I hate it when people I love condemn me.

"Listen," I said, "I gotta go see where Ray is."

Things changed. Every obvious thing and a lot of others changed, once I got my acceptance and full scholarship from Norfolk.

Some of those things, you could probably guess. I didn't have to sweat anymore. For anything. Grades came easy. Not wonderful grades, but my usual, just north of mediocre grades. But they came now without my having to break my neck or crack a book over them. It was made obvious, as it is for most graduating senior athletes, that I was no longer a priority, good or bad, of the education side of the education system. As long as I showed the proper respect, attended classes, stayed awake, answered whatever meatball question was tossed my way, I would do all right for the rest of my high school days.

I could go with that system.

I got along, and got along well. Got along with staff, with teachers and lunch ladies. Got along with guys, with athletes I knew before but knew better now, guys who were studs at basketball, or even guys who played sports that didn't matter, like tennis. I got along with smart kids who did stuff like debate, as well as with guys who sat around glassy-eyed and famously did nothing at all.

And this, I found, pleased me more than I ever would have guessed. Because a lot of guys in my position would have gone all stick-assed about it, noses in the air over the attentions of geeks and stoners and hall monitors. A lot of guys—and I have to criticize a lot of my colleagues in the sports world generally and football specifically here—figure that much of the regular free-range world is beneath us, and that if people want to like you then you might as well spit on them.

But here's what I found out. I *liked* being liked.

I mean, I really, really liked it when people liked me. I didn't necessarily want to be buddies with people, call them up and have them call me up and go to the movies together and all that. That took *involvement*, which, to be honest, I didn't do very well. But to have people think the right side up about me. Felt nice. To come home and recount to my dad, hey Ray, you have a kid who is liked, practically all over the board. That felt pretty okay.

Which is why, now that I had emerged out the other side of all the awfulness of the crippling, I could tell you—that was the worst, the worst hell-on-earth ever, and I'd sooner die than feel like that again. It meant more than a little, then, and if the investigations came down at the end and said I was some kind of beastman, I don't know what I would have done, but I would have done something quite unlovely, I guarantee you that. Because I knew all along I was a good guy, and to be declared otherwise would have been criminal. It would have battered me.

But it didn't, which is why life got so damn, damn good when it didn't. I was just so happy that it was decided officially that I wasn't bad. That it would be okay to like me. I know a guy's not supposed to care overly much about what other people think of him, but I do care a lot.

Even he understood. The guy. The kid. The unlucky

receiver. He knew how important that was. That he understood. He told me so. I received a card, which I kept. I would have framed it, if people wouldn't have gotten the wrong idea about it. It was just so important to me. As it is, I refer to it often. I even sent him a thank-you card for making me feel better.

And he understood everything, which a lot of people might not have.

Like the loosening up. That was one of the first, most surprising differences when things started turning right. Everybody loosened up, almost as soon as I returned to school.

It was as if somebody passed a law or a judgment, threw a switch, or opened a cage, releasing the problem and setting everybody free from it.

"Yo, Killer," Quarterback Ken said that first day, after word spread that I got my scholarship and had, in fact, turned down two others. Quarterback Ken, himself headed on a full boat to New Mexico State, launched the name, making it official. "Way to go, Killer."

What? How could that be? Who could that be? How could we have gotten here? Killer? Killer? K-i-l-l-e-r.

Me. Killer, me. How far from home was that word, nesting with me?

Killer Keir.

I was stunned at first, then embarrassed, then scared of

it, what it was, what it said about me, about them, about everything there is.

But before long, it settled. It became like a different thing, like something that had shocked me because of the surprise of it. Like fifty thousand people screaming "happy birthday" at you at once would surprise you if it was not even your birthday.

But it was their surprise, their welcome back, their celebration that no, things were not so scary and hellish after all, and *I* was not so scary and hellish after all, and if they could make fun of it, out-bogey the bogeyman, then we would all be okay.

Well, not all of us, exactly. And not okay, exactly. But he understood. Great bastard, he understood. I like to think that if it ever happened to me, I would understand as well. I would like to be a great bastard too.

It was something prepared, something accepted, something released like a great big ball of balloons into the sky, saying everything was all right now because somebody somewhere, up there, had ruled that it was, after all, all right now. It was official. *Officially* all right.

By lunchtime that day it had even become a rhyming thing, which it would remain thereafter.

Killer. Kill*eer*.

Rhymes with Keir. Keir Killeer.

I might have been able to stop it, at some point that

day. Stop it instead of blushing, as I did the first time, instead of nodding silently, as I did later, instead of laughing, as I did later still.

I could have done something in there to stop it, that first day, before it got too far along. There'd be no stopping it, after that first day. I could have done it, if only I were a different kind of guy.

But I'm not. I'm exactly this kind of guy. I'm all I've got, and I never claimed to have anything better to work with.

Ray took me out to a place, our place, to celebrate. It always pleased me that we were the kind of guys who had a place, and it pleased me further that the place was Manolo's Maison Meat. We'd always come here, but came a lot more often once the girls were out of the house and Risk was occupying the dining room table. Manolo's, as the name suggested, was a house of meat. You could get other stuff splashed around your big yellow tile plate to keep the meat company, but there was never any disputing the fact that this was a temple to killing stuff and wasting as little of it as possible. Ray and I were Manolo's keenest disciples.

It should have been all fun, all joy. And it was, up to a point. But it was more than that. The college issue meant, really, that things as we knew them were going to end, for good.

"I worry, though, Dad."

He took a drink of his glass of beer. He always called it that, a glass of beer. Never a beer, a brew, suds, or anything else. He always made it sound just slightly gentle, genteel, even though it was just beer, and even if he was drinking it from a bottle or a can.

"Would you like a glass of beer, Keir?" he'd asked.

"I'd love one, Ray," I'd answered.

I loved us together. I really loved us together.

"What would you possibly have to worry about?" he asked. "This is *it*, boy, the tip-top of life. Life is being good to you, because you have been good to it, and so you should enjoy it. You have nothing to worry about."

He popped a small handful of smokehouse almonds into his mouth and smiled at me broadly. He was wearing his suit. He has a few of them, but this is the one he wears, on the rare occasions he wears a suit. It looks like it was made from the skins off of Spanish peanuts, slick shiny thin-skin brown.

He looked a freakin' million, pardon my French.

"I worry . . . you're going to miss me."

"Ach," he said. Ach. His term of dismissal. And shyness, embarrassment, and love. Ach.

"Ach yourself," I said. "You're going to miss me, I think. You need me, old man."

"Ya, I need you, like February needs another *R*."

He was still smiling when he attempted to drain his glass. He couldn't stop grinning, so he couldn't drink his glass of beer because bits of it would come streaming out the corners of his mouth and land on his Spanish peanut suit.

Drained a lot of others though, eventually. We both did.

And we ate a pile of food. This is what it can be like, when it's me and Ray and nobody to stand between us and a defenseless supply of eats. It can be scary. Ray got the rib ticklers, a spread of rib-region remains of all the usual unfortunate farmyard beasts—spare ribs, baby-back ribs, country-style ribs, and a mini rack of lamb. I got Manolo's signature dish, the Noah's Ark, consisting of two of every animal he could get his hands on that day: marinated turkey breasts, pan-fried catfish, sirloin tips, a double ice-cream scoop of his pulled pork, and ostrich steak strips.

Dirty rice. Greens. Barbecue beans. All of it, still tasting somehow of meat. Even the sweet potato pie we had for dessert contained, I think, little bits of chicken. Mason jars filled with ice water, though they went pretty much undrunk.

Which you could not say about old Ray and young Keir.

"You know, they're going to ask you to do it again," he

said as he reached across to my plate and removed a big wedge of sirloin that had been left unattended just a little too long.

"Was I done with that?" I asked him.

"Ya, I think you were."

He ordered more glasses of beer.

"You know it," he said. "They'll be asking you to do more of it."

"Who they, and more of what, Dad?"

"They, being the school, the coaches . . ."

I had it worked out now.

"What, Dad, they're gonna expect me to cripple some-body again, is that what you're saying? They going to want me to cripple somebody every week?"

"Keir," he said slowly, calmly, clutching his beer tightly for balance, "coaches, other players, some loudmouth in the stands . . . you'll hear things. People will say stuff, you'll hear stuff . . . that's all."

That's all.

"What do you mean, Ray? That's all? That's not all. That's not even the end of a story. How can that be all?"

"Just be yourself, is all I'm saying," he said, his voice and manner growing thicker by the minute. "Right? Don't let circumstances control what happens to you. Be who you are, don't be who you not are. . . ."

He caught himself there, raised a hand to his mouth as

if he had burped, droopily smiled at me with his eyes.

"Don't you worry about it, Ray. I'm already there. I know who I not are, and I not are a cornerback, okay? I'm a kicker. I am going there for a kicker's life, and if it was cornerbacking that helped me get there, then beautiful. But if they expect to see me sticking and sticking people all over the field . . . well, I am sorry if they are disappointed."

He nodded. He liked that. He was happy with that, but it wasn't quite all somehow.

"You're all soft on the inside, Keir. You're a big softy."

I took a gulp of water, pausing for effect.

"Oh, ya," I said, "well guess what? I got a nickname now. At school. Wanna know what they're calling your boy now?"

"What?"

"Killer. That's right, me, the killer. What do you think of that?"

I could tell right off that he didn't think what he was supposed to think. He looked sadder than hell and started shaking his big Dad head.

"No," he said. "Make them stop calling you that, Keir. You know and I know that you are no kind of killer. You're a good boy."

I felt so bad, like I hurt his feelings or something, though how could that be? I just had to reach across the table and pat him on the side of his head.

"I know, Dad. People know. That's why it's such a joke. That's why I can get away with it, because it is so obviously not true."

Ray was only half relieved, and not even a little impressed.

"You aren't a hard man, and it wouldn't do you any favors to try and be. It's good that you're an old mush on the inside, and it would be even better to let people know that. Make them not call you Killer, Keir. Let them call you Mush instead."

"Shut up," I said. "I'm as tough as you ever were."

"Well, yes," he said, as if we were agreeing somehow.

Anyway, like I could stop it if I wanted to. The name was out now, it was mine, it was part of the world and I couldn't reverse the world.

"I'll tell the girls," Ray said, pointing at me and grinning slyly. "Do Fran and Mary know about this awful nickname of yours? *They'll* fix your wagon." He thought he was joking.

"Christ, Dad, don't do that."

He thought I was joking. He laughed loud and slapped the table hard enough to make all the plates and glasses jump.

Ray sank his beer and I sank mine and we got two more without even asking.

"For the celebration," the waiter said, putting the

beers down and clearing away plates that looked cleaner than the dishwasher would have got them. "Manolo says congratulations."

It's not a very big town.

Dad and I drank appreciatively, even though we practically had to wake ourselves up to do it.

"You know," he said, leaning heavily over the table, "my doctor once called me, a long time ago, not long after your mother died, called me *quasi-alcoholic*. How's that? I said, what's that, like Quasimodo? And he said, just be careful. Just always be careful, Ray, he told me."

He hung there, his face, his intensely lined, magnificent cool face suspended above the table between us, and all I could do was stare. And all he could do was stare.

Until we both took to our bottles and sipped.

"Ach," he said, refreshed, "but that was a long time ago. It went away. And I was careful."

I watched and watched him, waiting for a payoff, a tip, a laugh, or a frown, but instead he went blank on me, staring at me, as hard as a person can stare at a person, but still sidestepping me completely.

"You okay, old dude?" I asked.

His pilot light was relit. "Let's go visit your mother. Want to?"

It was closing in on midnight, a school night. We had a week's worth of food in our bellies and a month of alcohol in our blood. The cemetery in question goes all the way back to the Revolution days, and it is so gothic, crumbling, and overgrown in the older parts that ghosts are too afraid to go there. Even in the daytime.

Sometimes, oftentimes, I don't even miss my mother. She was the one who opted to die, not me. It was an effort for me to remember even a scrap about her, and this was not coldness, but just fact. I love my mother, love the idea of her and whatever vestiges of her I can still feel in me, in Fran and Mary. But really, honestly, fairly, I love her through Ray. You cannot help loving my mother, missing my mother, when you see the love and the lonesome that cracks like lightning across his face when he hears her name, no matter how many heavens away she is by now.

I once, just once, expressed a small lack of enthusiasm for the idea of visiting her grave on a Thanksgiving Day when the Lions were playing the Cowboys on TV and my body was overdosed with that chemical in turkey that makes you all sleepy.

I didn't hear his voice directed at me for four solid days.

If ever I was going to not hear his voice again, it would be because one of us was dead. Preferably me.

I hate it when people I love are silent to me.

"Sure, Dad," I said. "Let's go see Mom. Who's driving?"

"We'll take turns," he said, pulling me up out of my

chair, all renewed, happy, and energized, like we were a couple of kids off on some great adventure.

It was almost noon when I woke up after the night out with my parents.

The house reeked, and my head rang with fire engine alarms until I slithered downstairs and swallowed some Tylenol with a quart of orange juice.

I walked around aimlessly. Dad was long gone. He never missed work, ever, not even if a train hit him.

Tougher than I will ever be, my dad.

I went to the dining room, where Risk still sat.

Apparently, we had played. When we came in? Jesus, yes, we had. Ray kicked my butt all over Asia, the rat. Took advantage of me while I was vulnerable. He could always function under the influence, under any and all influences, while I, most definitely, could not. My decisions, my memory, my brain control, deserted me at the hour of need.

I was a lucky guy, in fact, that my dad was easygoing on the issue of partying, because I could never fool anybody if I had had a bit too much to drink or whatever. He caught me one time when I had a shot of peppermint schnapps at a freshman party, and he did it without even smelling me. He caught me over the phone, when I called to say I would be staying at a friend's house instead of coming home, if that was all right with him.

He laughed out loud.

I came home.

Now he was at work, and I was wandering the empty house in my underwear, waiting for the Tylenol to soothe me and the orange juice to rehydrate me before I made my next move, if in fact I had a next move in me.

I would never do this again. Never again.

I remembered. I remembered crying. It was not a dream. I was crying, out loud, with sounds and tears and everything, and Dad had to pat me on the back and tell me everything was going to be all right.

It was at the cemetery. Possibly.

Or during Risk. And there may have been some vomit.

How does he do it? How does he just do it? How does he get through everything?

School was obviously out of the question. But I was going to football practice if it killed me.

Soft on the inside? I may not have been the Killer, but I could be at least a shadow of the man my dad was.

S ometimes you get caught. Caught up in moments, in the whirlwind of events. Caught unawares. It's just not you but wrong place, wrong time, wrong company can really easily add up to giving people the wrong idea about yourself. And yet again the way things look drift away from the way things really are.

I had become, in my senior year, a somebody, and let's face it, much of it had to do with the whole "Killer" thing, which erected a rugged new structure on the formerly vacant lot of my persona. Like I said, I was liked around school, and I liked being liked. I had all the football teammates and the soccer teammates—because I played intramural spring soccer, strictly to keep in shape for football, and not because I saw the point of soccer whatsoever. And I had the hundreds of other casual friends I'd made in my travels, all happy to slap my back or offer a cup or three of kindness behind the stands after school. I considered this popularity, and I considered popularity pleasant.

The season had already been filled with many gatherings, many good-byes and best wishes, and many fine nights out. The football team had a final breakup party, which basically involved a dinner at the coach's brother's restaurant, followed by three hours hanging out at the field in the dark, followed by another hour of more industrious breaking up. We broke up couples in cars down by the river. We broke up windows at the library. And we broke up a statue of Paul Revere and the other guy who rode with him but nobody seems to remember.

Here's what can happen: You can look at a thing and at the time it will look funny, if conditions are right. In the mean light of day an event from the night before might look plain nasty, but that does not automatically render it nasty, in its context. Even if I might partway agree with you about the nastiness in the light, that still doesn't mean that at its original time the thing itself couldn't have been a very different, better thing.

We thought of ourselves as crusaders for righteousness at the time, because we really did a job on Paul R. while leaving the other guy—who I still cannot quite remember—pretty much intact. We thought it was a statement somehow for the underdog, at the time. We saw ourselves as freedom fighters and rascals at the same time, the kind of guys people talk about for generations to come in that great, "lovable rogue" kind of way. Who would not love to be remembered as a lovable rogue? I could not imagine such a person.

The locals could. The local townsfolk didn't see our correction of history in quite the same light, so a big hoo-ha was made out of it, and the underclassmen, as dictated by our school's fine tradition, stepped up and took all the blame. Several received quite a public paddling for all the high spirits, and two were even given a bit of community service.

They couldn't see the spirit of the thing, the locals. You can't simply go by what you see, without seeing the spirit. That kind of attitude is inexcusable.

I went back to the statues the next day. It was a goddamn mess. It was a pitiful, brainless mess. I stood there, mortified, trying to pull together the two planets, the one where we were just guys, just having fun saying good-bye to ourselves, our team, our younger and less responsible selves, and this putrid stinking planet here where everything was nothing because some animals brought everything down to nothing. I could not imagine being on both planets. I couldn't be part of both worlds.

Something went wrong. Something happened beyond what happened. Because I swear to you that the scene of the daylight was far beyond what I saw the night before. Somebody had to have come back and made it all worse.

Because we didn't mean to do this. I swear, I would remember if we toppled the whole statue over. Paul Revere was lying in bits, four, five big chunks as well as all the little ones, him and his horse all blended up into one hideous mythological beast of chaos. Who would do that?

And the other guy. We were trying to make a statement. A small statement, maybe, a stupid statement, maybe, but a statement of some kind. Why would we go and mess up the other guy? Why the hell would we go and cut the head off the other guy? That ruined everything. That . . . emptied everything of any sense at all. We wouldn't ever be lovable rogues after that because that was too far. Too goddamn far. Nobody would ever confess, either, you can bet on that. I mean, I wouldn't be surprised if some other bunch got there after us and really did all the stuff after all. But we'll never know, because nobody would ever admit it. There are some real jerks in this town, you know.

Dawes. I went up in the mean light of day and read the base and found out that Revere's pal was Dawes. I probably wouldn't forget it anymore.

The other breakup party I went to was for the soccer team. I was there because I was made an honorary member, by virtue of my playing spring intramural soccer with some of the varsity and playing it pretty damn well, I must say, combined with the fact that most first-string football players wouldn't give soccer the time of day. And I was the Killer. I brought them some badly needed cred and in return they provided me with a good workout and a surprisingly good time—though I never said that in mixed company.

An altogether more subdued and dignified affair, the soccer team breakup. As long as it remained the soccer team. Until the football team, or some football-team-shaped figures wearing balaclavas, arrived on a not-so-anonymous tip. They showed up in the parking lot for another session of high-spirited hijinks, leading to the traditional temporary, all-in-fun kidnapping of a few neatly dressed soccer players for a few hours of late-night involuntary skinny-dipping for the video camera. And really, it was funny, funny, funny, even to the soccer players involved, who were great sports about the whole thing and had a great laugh about it.

That was how I saw it. That was how I remembered it.

Except that, later, days later, none of that, the good time good stuff, managed to get onto the tape. The tape, who knows, the tape missed most of the funny stuff, or got edited, or got too much water on it, but all the greatness of the event, the fun, the camaraderie of sportsmen having a laugh all together, all of that got wiped off somehow, and some grotesque, awful, dark, blurry horror film got on there instead. Who was doing the filming? I couldn't remember. Whoever it was, they sucked. They ruined the tape, and ruined the time for everybody who was there. They pointed at all the wrong things and missed all the best. They were too blurry on what was great. They were too clear on one or two things that weren't.

I only even knew it was the right film because I thought I saw me. I thought. It was me. I thought. Looked like a soccer player. I was a soccer player. What was a soccer player doing there with the football players? Acting like a football player? Not a kicker, either, but a *football* player. Doing football player stuff. It wasn't me. It looked like me, but like I said it was out of focus and very dark and jerky and all over the place. But whoever he was, this guy was a busy guy. He wasn't content on the sidelines. He wasn't content with naked embarrassed soccer players. He had to go down into the water and make sure they took long hard pulls off a bottle. You couldn't see that the bottle was Jack Daniels, but if you knew Jack Daniels you could tell. You could tell from the squareness of the bottle and from the way the kid juddered like electroshock after he drank it. Soccer players can't drink. Then, even in his suit, he had to make sure he herded them all like sheep back into the cold water while the football players whooped and whooped, and then for some God-knows reason he had to shove their heads under the water for a good long time.

The guy with the camera—who I could kill if I could ever figure out who it was—while he couldn't quite manage to get hardly any of the good fun parts, then had the presence of mind to swing around in time to catch a bunch of football guys pissing on each of the little tidy mounds of the soccer players' dressing-up, going-out clothes. That they'd worn. For their big dinner.

One of the few true things that useless tape did show was that I was *not* one of those pissing football players.

Now I think I didn't make it onto the tape at all. Probably I was too boring, too out of the way, or not bad enough for the filmmaker's taste. And anyway, I was a soccer player too, honorary or not. How could I do stuff like that to members of the soccer team if I was a member of the soccer team? That's why I couldn't have.

I was there because they invited me. I was there because they liked me. So I couldn't have.

I remembered, earlier that evening, being a soccer player, at a soccer dinner, eating soccer player food with soccer players on either side of me, finishing somebody's broccoli while he finished my roast potato.

Broccoli, even. The evidence was right there on the plate. Bad guys don't eat broccoli, and they certainly don't help another guy finish his. I saw a good guy there. The film saw other things, entirely.

Did I mention that I watched the tape with a room full of guys and beer and noise, laughing and clapping? We watched the same way we had watched scores of tapes of other football teams, trying to work out what made them tick. Maybe I didn't mention it because I forgot. Maybe I forgot because the whole time, the sound of the volume of the room was off for me. Dead silent. And because I was feeling kind of sick.

BECAUSE OF GIGI BOUDAKIAN

Here is another reason why I could not have done what she says I did. I was always my best when I was with her. I went to the prom with her. How 'bout that. Even after it happened I couldn't fully believe it happened. I would be happy to one day have my headstone read, BORN . . . DIED . . . WENT TO THE PROM WITH GIGI BOUDAKIAN.

I could have taken the limo driven by my dad's cousin Rollo, but there were problems with that. Rollo, being a professional limousine driver, had most likely seen everything a human can possibly get up to, and would hardly notice me, and if he did notice probably wouldn't tell. But then he might. And if there happened to be any damage to his car . . .

Which is not to say that I had any intention of getting

involved in unseemly behavior that would get me in hot water, even with my very forbearing dad during the night of my once-in-a-lifetime senior prom.

But I could hope.

And hope's name was Gigi Boudakian, and we were not in love at the time. Or, rather, she was, but it was with an air force man named Carl stationed a short but inconvenient plane ride away who could not get back to enjoy the festivities, and so sent word that anybody else who attempted to would have their nuts blown off with a U.S. government-issue rifle. I was safe from that, however, because Carl and I had been friends for exactly as long as Gigi and I had been friends, which was a trustworthy long time. Gigi's father, who was a well-known, well-connected, major money carpet dealer in town was understood to have pretty much the same feelings on the matter, only substitute ceremonial sword for rifle, while the nuts part remained unchanged. And me and Mr. Boudakian also lacked that critical several years' friendship.

I got the okay to take Gigi because of Quarterback Ken, with whom we would be double-dating in his father's Lexus. Ken was out of the Gigi running as a potential boyfriend from the beginning, as a result of his being a blood relation of the Boudakians in some distant way that would not have prompted Ken to remove *himself* from the running, but there you go. And now he had a kind of a bombshell girlfriend of his own. I was deemed suitable because Mr. Boudakian felt the Sarafian-ness of my father's surname cancelled out the MacTavish-ness of my mother's, and because he didn't know about the O'Brian half of my dad that made things 3-1 against my Armenian-ness, but since it was a wholly unfair system anyway I felt justified in shutting up about it. And because Gigi and I had been on friendly and honorable terms during the whole time of her serious relationship with her true love Carl, I could be counted on not to try anything.

I tried everything.

Within reason. I am a gentleman. But I did find myself, throughout what was all in all a really lovely evening, making a minor nuisance of myself. I couldn't help it, hadn't planned it, did not approve of it, but carried on with it. We danced, and that was fine. Ate, and that was fine. When they came around with the traditional beef-or-turkey question, the staff didn't even flinch when I told them, both. And they took me seriously, *gave* me both. In food terms, this was the greatest date I ever had. I nearly called Ray to tell him about it right there on the spot and have him come see.

The music was not good but not a problem, conversation was consistently light, funny, rude within reason. Everybody I knew was there, everybody dressed to the moon. Everybody was everybody's best buddy, everybody was exuberant, and everybody wanted everybody else's date.

Except me. I couldn't even imagine wanting any other date on this night. And I have a pretty buzzy imagination.

The problem was, she couldn't keep her hands off me.

Couldn't keep her hands off my hands, actually. When we danced, her hands did most of the dancing, flittering up and down her back, sides, hips, pursuing my hands like squirrels chasing each other up and down a tree. Somehow, it seemed every place I put them was an inappropriate place, so I had to keep moving them, and then the way I was moving them became the problem, so you can appreciate that Gigi Boudakian was being a little difficult to deal with.

At the table it was more of the same. She was holding my wrist with one hand while holding her idle fork with the other. Then she was elbowing me. Then she was whipping out her cell phone and dialing . . .

"What, what, what?" I said pleadingly, folding my hands prayerlike and earning a reprieve.

"You are drunk, Keir," she said.

"No," I said seriously.

"Yes," she said.

"Not really," I said.

"Yes, really," she said.

"A little."

"A lot."

Hmm.

"Well, everybody is drunk."

"Not everybody."

"Everybody."

"Not me."

"Well, whose fault is that?"

"Listen, Keir..." she said, and there wasn't a tremendous amount of suspense about where this was headed, since she had her phone out and buttons beeping as she spoke.

"I'm sorry," I said into her free ear.

She looked up at me with a hard, penetrating, not unkind or unfair look.

She was so decent. She was lovely and sharp and she was smart and classic. I suddenly felt like I had been wiping my hand on my sleeve, shouting obscenities, fighting, pissing in the punch bowl. She was great. She was lovely and decent, and so, so deserving of all the best things, and would surely wind up with them later on, in college, in love, in the carpet business or on Broadway, in life, if she could get through the degradation of this.

"Please, please don't leave," I said. "Please. Please."

She looked at me harder still.

"Please."

Damn, she could look at you a long, cold minute.

"Get it together," she said firmly.

I felt like the luckiest guy there. I got it together, while Gigi Boudakian and I never did. Though I never stopped thinking about it.

All the sweeter. All the sweeter it was, then, when we danced, for as long as they'd let us, and we went up to the

Blue Hills Reservation with everybody else, and had a couple of drinks, silly drinks, harmless drinks, sloe gin fizzy drinks, we made a fire, even, and told stories, even, and our mighty tuxedoes and shiny gowns took on ever more dramatic and unnatural forms in the dancing firelight, and Gigi Boudakian stayed there right next to me and listened along with me as we all told stupid and heroic stories about one another, about four years of one another, and other couples, real couples who were supposed to be together and knew they would be together and had their plans planned for months and their pockets stuffed with condoms and pills and whatever, slipped off, two by two and even four by four and I, of course, started getting hungry all over again, and hunger making me bold, I asked Gigi Boudakian if she would go with me to the International House of Pancakes.

And you know what? Do you know what?

No, actually, she did.

We dismissed Quarterback Ken and his Lexus and his date, who was an older lady who had actually had her own senior prom two years before, but that's quarterback life for you. Well, actually, they dismissed themselves, but we didn't mind, not at all, because it was a wonderful thin-air breezy walk, down out of the hills and two miles toward town to get to the IHOP, and when Gigi Boudakian took off her shoes because no way no how were those heels making that trek, I took mine off too because it seemed to be the thing to do and when finally you snap out of it and realize you are with a person like Gigi Boudakian, you *do* the thing to do.

She appreciated that, Gigi did, and I believe it helped her to relax more, and to forget some of the things I might have been trying earlier in the night, and remember some of what it was that made us cool and easy friends all that time before and led us directly to this point, to this moment, this *now* of our lives.

Things were clear when we came within sight of the pancake house. My head was clear, the air was clear, it was early morning in that unspeakable great gap in between the night people giving it up and the day people taking it over, in that luscious pink-orange spring morning light that you worry, if you're like me, that maybe you don't deserve, that maybe you are stealing, spoiling for everyone, by being out at this hour.

It was in that light that Gigi Boudakian took my hand.

She didn't *slap* my hand. She didn't seize my wrist. She slipped her hand into mine, mine into hers, so softly, so easily, that my reaction was to pull away and apologize.

"Ah, sorry about that," I said.

She laughed. My sweet lord, such a sound. Made me wonder, momentarily, why I ever wanted to get a girl to do anything else but laugh.

They had to ask us to put our shoes back on when we entered the pancake house because we forgot and stood there stupidly by the PLEASE WAIT TO BE SEATED sign with our shoes in one hand and each other in the other. But they asked us politely, even sweetly. Like there was something charmed and charming at work, and we were all of us in it together.

That's the way people all over the restaurant looked at us, very nice, very soft, very tilt-the-head-and-smile because, I guess, we had prom written all over us and we reminded them of other stuff, good stuff, their stuff maybe and their friends' stuff, way old stuff, and more recently their kids' own stuff, if it went well and didn't wind up all smutty and slutty and bloody and dead like a lot of prom nights seem to, and like this one obviously did not.

It was, too, all the good stuff of prom legend. This is what was supposed to happen, the barefoot sweetness and pancake house at dawn and nobody getting hurt or dirty, but instead giving off an unmistakable whiff of finer love things.

I lied to you earlier. I lied earlier because I loved Gigi Boudakian when I said I didn't. I just didn't know it before the International House of Pancakes sat us by the window, by the parking lot, by the parkway, by ourselves.

I ordered pigs in blankets. Side of bacon. Coffee. Cranberry juice. Didn't order toast, but they brought some, and little packets of jelly. Gigi Boudakian had an omelette with cheese and green peppers.

The food came, and I could not believe how good her

order looked and smelled. Caught me completely by surprise. They put hash browns there too, on the side, bumped up against the omelette, even though I did not hear her ask them to do that.

"You want to trade?" I asked her.

"No, I do not," she said. "That's why I ordered this"— she pointed at her food with her knife, in the most attractive way, the most, I mean, kill-me beautiful way of gesturing—"instead of that." She pointed at my plate. A whole different gesture entirely.

I was wearing a smile then, must have been pretty goofy from the way it felt.

"I'm thinking that you're a pretty friggin' great girl, you know," I said.

She cut a neat perfect wedge of egg, reached across the table with her fork, and used her knife to gently slide the bite onto my plate.

"That's all you're getting," she said.

I ate it, still smiling, still watching her.

"That's a pretty friggin' great egg, too."

She smiled, tucked another prim little wedge of that egg into the gentle upturned corner of her mouth. We ate, mostly silently, but altogether pleasantly, comfortably, for as long as it took me to finish off a small herd of blanketed pigs. Which wasn't long. I was staring out the window, content and pleased and politely not watching Gigi Boudakian eat, seeing the parkway wake up with cars, sipping my coffee, when she asked.

"Are you okay, Keir? With what you did? To that boy?"

I swung my head around, the way a crane moves from one site to another. I looked, wide-eyed, forcing her further just to do it, just to make her meet me in the middle of where she wanted me to go.

"Huh?"

"You know, Keir. The whole 'Killer' thing. It must bother you. I know it must bother you."

I looked back out the window. Not to be dramatic or anything, but just to look back out the window.

"You know," I said, "it doesn't. It doesn't bother me, much. Bothered me before, bothered me at first. But really . . . really, it doesn't bother me now. Like you would think it might. Like *you*, obviously, think it does."

I finished my talking, and my looking out the window, and faced her directly, waiting.

"Okay," said Gigi Boudakian, with a shrug. "I just wondered. If it hurt, you know?"

"No," I said. "I hit him just right."

"That's not what I—"

I raised a hand. "I know what you meant. See, I heard from him, you know? Got a card and everything. We're okay. He says it's okay. Says *I'm* okay, okay? So it's okay."

I didn't know there just what I was doing, but I was doing something, because a wave of trembly came up over

Gigi Boudakian's face and back down again, and she reached over the table and put a warm hand over my coffee-warm hand and tilted her head sadly.

I looked at her hand, I looked at her. I asked, "You want to meet him? I could take you to meet him, maybe. He'd like to see me sometime I think, and he'd *love* to see you anytime, who wouldn't?"

She pulled her hand back and pulled herself back a bit, to her side of the table, but not so I felt like a creep.

"I couldn't," she said. "You mean, now? Anyway . . . whatever, no, I couldn't. No. Thank you, Keir."

I leaned way over now, over her plate, even, which was not very mannerly, but I wouldn't stay long.

"Do you love me?" I asked.

"No," she said matter-of-factly.

I leaned back, away from her plate.

"I knew that."

"Yes, you did."

"You like me, though?"

"Yes, I do."

"I knew that."

"You know what I think?" Gigi Boudakian said, pushing her plate out into the dangerous deep water of the middle of the table where I could get at her scraps of egg and hash brown and large corners of toast that were way more than crusts.

"Let me guess: You think you love me after all."

"Well, no. What I think is, I think you weren't so wild, you weren't so . . . difficult, when you weren't the Killer."

For this I stopped eating. Stopped chewing, with food in my mouth.

"That's what you think?"

She nodded sympathetically.

"Jeez, I wasn't even close, was I?"

She shook her head.

"It's just a name," I said.

No response.

"He said it was okay. He said everything was okay, I was okay. You'll see in the card he sent me, you'll see."

She nodded.

I returned to eating. There wasn't much left on either plate but crumbs, snail trails of grease and butter, jelly daubs.

"You think I'm wild?" I asked.

"Kind of."

"But you still like me."

She gave me something of a how-sad smile. You know, the one that comes with the sideways tilt of the head.

"Do you still remember, in kindergarten? My joke?"

Like it was yesterday.

"Not sure I do, actually," I said.

"Sure you do." She started giggling. "My mother was walking us to school like she did, and it was very cold. I had on my big parka. Oh, come on, you do."

It was robin's egg blue, the parka. With tawny flecked fake rabbit fur around the hood and cuffs.

I sighed, like I was bothered. "I think I recall some distant memory of you getting me to look into your sleeve because you said your hand had gone missing."

Now she was laughing. She covered her mouth with both hands, but was pretty clearly audible anyway.

"I'm so sorry, Keir," she said, pulling off the miracle of sounding truly sorry and delirious with laughter at the same time.

"What?" I said now, and had to laugh myself. "For punching me in the face? For taking advantage of my trusting nature?"

I was only making it worse. She could hardly form words. "Yes," she said, nodding frantically. "You were so sweet."

"No, I wasn't, I was just stupid."

"That is not true," she said, calming down and grabbing both my hands in hers. "And you never even tried to get me back."

"I think I was just afraid you would beat me up."

She looked up close and all the way in at me. "No, you weren't," she said. "You just didn't have it in you. And it was right then that I started *almost* loving you."

It had to be possible for her to feel the thunder of my heartbeat through the contact of our hands. I pulled away, but she could probably still feel it through the floor.

"Like you do now," I said.

"Now and always, as always," she said warmly.

Almost loved. To be almost loved. To be almost loved by Gigi Boudakian.

What a wonder was that? What a horror was that? I was so proud ecstatic grateful angry I felt for that instant I knew what it was like to be fire.

"Ya," I said, standing and very politely wiping the corners of my mouth with my yellow paper napkin, "well, I was very happy when your mother smacked you."

"Who are you kidding?" she said, standing across the table from me like a gunslinger. "She only did that when you started crying."

There was nothing left that the International House of Pancakes could do for us, so we left. The morning was still so beautiful, soft and dewy and warm, that we tried to finish what we started and walk all the way home. But that was just not practical, not possible, not a very good idea.

The world was waking up, the spell was lifting, and we were coming down. Things were starting not to feel the way they felt before. Every step was heavier than all the earlier steps. We carried our shoes again, but the pavement was getting hotter, harder, grittier. Sweat stains were blooming under the arms of my shirt and were even trying to fight their way all the way through the mighty polyester rented jacket. Worst, worst of all, sweat dared to appear under the arms of Gigi Boudakian where sweat should never ever be, creeping down her sides like poison ivy staining a lovely satin garden wall.

We were getting so, so tired. The sun, which a while ago was a sunrise, was now my evil nemesis.

"I'll get a cab, huh?" I said.

"I thought you would never ask."

What I would like right here is to tell you about how, in that cab, I didn't try anything, not right in the closing moments of the greatest night, the finest memorable prom night, with the wondrous Gigi Boudakian. How I treated her with the respect and adoration she deserved. And I would like to tell you that she loved me beyond almost.

This is the problem. This is what Gigi does not understand. Things have conspired, to cloud her mind. She's not a drinker, Gigi. Some people shouldn't drink. It is understandable, but she has just got it wrong. Some of it is cloud, some of it is misunderstanding, but all of it is wrong, and all of it can be straightened out. It has to be straightened out.

"We just need to talk," I say. "Please, can't we talk?"

"No, we cannot."

"It's practically not even light out yet."

"It's light enough. Let me go. You have to let me go."

"Okay, Gigi. What if, even if I didn't, I said all right, you're right, whatever. What if I did that and then I said it so you can feel all right, and we can just leave it there, leave it right here in this room behind us when we leave, and nobody, not Carl and not my father and not your father or anybody, has to be involved or upset about it? What about that, and then, like I said, we can leave it behind us, close the door on it, and you can feel all right and we can get on with stuff. What if I did that for you?

"Because I am sorry, Gigi. Whether I did something or I didn't, I am sorry because of how you feel about it. How you feel and how you feel about me."

She tries the doorknob again, and I grab her wrist with both hands.

I have both hands tight on Gigi Boudakian's lovely soft long wrist. She looks up at me, almost as if she is afraid of me. Things are so wrong.

"Please, Keir," she says, and her voice is a shaky whisper. She looks down at my hands holding her wrist, and Gigi Boudakian's tears drop, right onto the back of my hand, and this is a nightmare now. I should be the one crying.

Things are so, so, so wrong.

Something changed in those weeks and months heading out of my high school life. Things were different. I was different. Physically different.

After football and soccer seasons were behind me and party season was in full session, I became aware of myself and my appetites. Myself *as* appetite.

But like I said, something changed. During the last half of the last year of high school, my body started treating life differently. I kept up with my hunger, my thirst, my desires of all kinds, kept them all going at a fairly high level, but my bod shifted down a gear.

My boyishness, which I had come to rely on, started to desert me.

My waistline had the nerve to protrude. "What have we got here?" I said to myself out loud as I stood naked in front of my freestanding, full-length, oak-framed mirror, as I was wont to do. My father got me the mirror for my birthday. I had requested it.

I stared at it full-on. Turned sideways, then sideways the other way. Hell.

"Ray," I called.

He came quickly down the hall, opened the door, found me there.

He stood with his hands on his hips, shaking his head at me, as I stared at me.

"You've got to get yourself a girlfriend, soon," he said.

"I'm fat, Ray."

He seemed a little surprised by this. We had been living alone, the pair of us, in bachelor conditions for a good while now. We were not shy or careful around each other. The house had its sights and sounds and smells, which we had gotten pretty good at not noticing, which the girls certainly would not have tolerated, but this here, me and the nakedness and the mirror and all, this was testing him.

"You are not fat. You're not so fine I want to see you naked, however. Get dressed."

He left me there, alone. Me and my body, alone. Me and my body and my gut, all squeezed into my room together, uncomfortably crowded. My lean frame, cornerback lean, kicker thin, soccer-player light and springy, suddenly mutated with this jiggly Jell-O mold grafted on around my beltline. I turned angrily away from the mirror, like it was the mirror's fault. It certainly wasn't mine.

But it was more than just that. I felt tired. And slow. And hurt. I had pulled a thigh muscle a couple of weeks before, just playing some casual basketball in gym class—nobody gets hurt in gym class—and it was refusing to heal.

I had to start training for real. I was going to get fit and stay fit. Something large, larger even than my belly, was coming over me.

It was over. This life, or this leg of it anyway, was over, and truth be told, I was not unhappy or unprepared for it. Except for living with my dad, there wasn't really any part of my life that I was not now prepared to trade in, trade up, for bigger and better things. Faster things, stronger things, prettier things, harder things, newer things, unknown things, and scarier things.

So when I came downstairs, I told my dad I would be skipping breakfast. And that was just the beginning. "I've been thinking, Ray, that I don't really want to have that open house here after graduation."

He stopped washing up and looked at me as if I had stripped again and was looking at my naked reflection in the breakfast plates.

"You?"

"Right."

"Keir MacTavish Sarafian?"

"Right."

"You know that open house actually means party? You know you are saying you don't want a party. Could that possibly be true?"

"Ya, Dad. I just feel like . . . I've had enough. Not that I don't still love a party. Just that . . . I think I've done it now. Like I have had the breakup parties and the going away parties, and most of all the good-bye stuff and, honestly, I just don't feel like doing it again."

I was briefly worried that Ray was going to be hurt. That he was going to feel bad that I had turned down his nice offer to throw me a do, that I had cut the legs off his big chance to send me off in style like he did for Mary and then Fran and that, I must say, he did spectacularly well. We were still pushing people out of the house two days later both times.

But he was okay. Which I should have known he would be.

"What do I want?" he said, lightly butting my head with his.

"You want what I want, Dad."

"That's right, goofus, and don't you forget it. So, what *do* you want? A trip to Bermuda or someplace, I suppose."

"No. All I want is Rollo."

He dried off his hands. "Rollo?"

"Ya, just Rollo."

"Really? Just Rollo, not his limousine?"

"Duh, Dad."

Ray's cousin, Rollo, owned what was by some distance the finest, gaudiest, most hysterically decked-out stretch limo in this area. You normally had to book him months in advance for a weekend. He was expensive, and only slightly moved by family considerations.

"And what exactly do you want with Rollo?"

"All I want is just to ride around. For a few hours. Tooling around. Seeing places, seeing people. Picking up a friend here and there, having a laugh, dropping them off again. Showing off. Doing only what I feel like doing, when the mood hits me. Taking a stretch limo through the KFC drive-through. Seeing who I want, when I want, skipping all the rest of it, then when I'm done with it, being done.

"And not getting up out of my seat the whole time."

He looked at me with great intensity, leaning up close. Like one of those pictures of the Kennedy brothers conferring over the Cuban Missile Crisis or Marilyn Monroe.

"Damn," he said with pride. "That's a plan."

As graduation approached I felt righter and righter about it. While a lot of people at school were preparing for parties— mostly by partying all the time—I was pulling back, slowing down, stepping away. And it felt good.

I found a new and brilliant method for getting in condition: I ate and drank less and exercised more. I found that—miracle—if I stretched regularly and correctly, my thigh muscle didn't hurt anymore. I started going out for long runs for the first time ever and discovered that I liked it. Not just the running, the *thump-thump-thump* of it, which could be boring as hell sometimes, and painful, and sick-inducing, but the touring element. Nearly every time I went out running in the weeks leading up to graduation, I felt like I was making my victory lap. I even began to have some kind of hazy fantasy, in which I had achieved something heroic and monumentally physical and was running around acknowledging the love and respect of the townspeople. I caught myself, on occasions, returning somebody's normal greeting wave with a big all-hail-Caesar wave of my own.

I hadn't done anything. I knew I hadn't done anything. All that was going on was the same thing that was going on for hundreds of other kids in town at the same time, that had gone on for thousands and thousands of other kids before us over the generations. I was finishing school, respectably but unspectacularly, and moving on away to college. I had done my time, had my times, and made my mark, although some might say my mark would have been better left unmade.

But that was past, and it was okay now.

I was starting to feel what was maybe an appropriate level of nostalgia for the old town. Passing my old ugly 1960s-style grammar school, I didn't feel the same cold and disagreeable urge to cross the street and pretend I never knew the place. I felt more like a benign, warming, safe appreciation for it, a feeling stoked by the completely unexpected return of a few good memories there. Same for the church I no longer attended. Same for the Hi-Lo supermarket, which had changed to the A & P, which had changed to Stop & Shop, all of which I worked for, however briefly.

Maybe, I thought—because I realized that I could have thoughts when I was running that I couldn't seem to have at any other time—this was all a sign that I was getting old. Getting old really, really fast, like Robin Williams in that movie *Jack.* I was having to watch my weight, I was getting nagging little old-man injuries (my arches were now hurting), and I was getting all wishy-washy about a place that I really would have told you just a few weeks ago didn't mean much more to me than hot meals, a nice house, and Ray.

But I wasn't getting old. In fact, if you asked most people, they'd say it was rare to even catch me acting my age.

No, it was simpler than that. Simpler and more boring and normal.

I was leaving. Leaving everything I had known, the place I was me, the people I had only ever known, and Ray.

And, I suspected, I wasn't coming back. Not really.

Mary came back a lot, for a while that first year. Then she came back less. Then Fran started college, started coming back for lots of weekends and holidays, and then, lots less. And with the two of them now already signed up for some summer study program in Wales, it was not too hard to see the center of things here kind of pulling loose from its moorings.

Maybe that's what was getting to me. Why should that be getting to me? I'd been happy to move on. Anxious, even. Except for Ray.

"What are you going to do, Ray?" I said without a word of explanation as I burst, sweaty and more breathy than necessary, through the door after my run.

I felt a little ridiculous when I saw him there, cool as a cuke, cool as Ray, sitting in front of the TV with a turkey sandwich in his hand and a beer at his feet. He was watching a home improvement show, which was a passion of his. He personally refused to ever lift a hammer, paint a brush stroke, or oil a hinge so shrieky with rust the neighbors must have suspected the old single dad had been beating his poor kids daily for decades.

"Look at the nonsense these guys waste precious life time on," Ray said, pointing half his sandwich like a gun at the tool-belt-wearing TV guy. "There are so much more important things to do with your life, if you got a life, than putting shelves and track lighting in your garage."

It was always this way. Always. He shook his sandwich hard at the guy, to try and shake him out of it. A slice of cucumber fell on the floor. I went over to him, picked it up off the floor, and ate it. Then I kissed him on top of his head. He had the very beginnings of a bald spot toward the back, exactly smacked-lips size.

"Going to take a shower, Dad," I said.

He waited until I was almost out of the living room.

"Going to buy another dog, probably, maybe," he said.

I stopped. "What?"

"You asked me what I was going to do. When you came in, there, you asked me."

He did not take his eyes from the TV, as if he were actually taking note of the instruction going on.

"Ya, right, but I didn't think you—"

"And maybe fix up the house. A little. With the extra time. I kind of let it go, over time. Over time."

I stood looking at him. He knew. He already knew what I was asking, what I was thinking. He was already thinking it. He was thinking it here, while I was thinking it out there, running.

"You had other stuff to do, Ray. You were busy."

"Yes I was," he said. "I was busy with other stuff."

I could not, for the moment, walk away. The sweat, clinging to me and cooling, felt awful, the way it could, felt like a thin skimming of drying cement all over my body. Talking wasn't much easier.

"Another dog?" I said.

"Ya. Maybe. Maybe something really small."

"That's good, Dad. That's good."

"That, and starting my other family, of course."

"Of course."

I cracked the cement, backed out of the room and partway up the stairs.

"Risk?" he called while simultaneously turning up the TV too loud.

"Of course," I called back. "When I come out."

"Fran called, wants you to call her back," he said even louder because the television was getting louder. He had accidentally left his thumb on the button, which was not as uncommon a thing as you might imagine.

"Take your thumb off the button, Dad," I yelled.

"Oh, right," he yelled back. The volume subsided. I took my shower.

When I came out, feeling newly skinned and light, I found, on the telephone table, a plate of cracker sandwiches left for me. Ray's specialty, Ritz crackers filled with crunchy peanut butter and raspberry jam with the gigantic seeds that snapped when you bit them.

Hmm. These were suspicious little treats. Snack sedatives that Dad used to whip up at times of duress. Sometimes my duress, sometimes his. Sometimes we just invented some duress that was nobody's.

I picked up the phone, sat in the chair, and dialed Norfolk.

"No, Fran," I said.

"Try to understand, Keir. I wanted to come. We both wanted to come—"

"Tomorrow, Fran. You are supposed to be here tomorrow. How can you be calling me today to say you are not coming tomorrow?"

"We just . . . you're right, we should have let you know sooner, but we were really trying to make it. We so wanted to be there, but exams, they're just killing us. We are studying every minute as it is, and I just don't see how we can be there at your graduation on Sunday and be ready and be here for the exams at eight o'clock Monday morning."

There was an extremely long pause.

"Are you going to talk to me?" she said.

I took one delicious Ritz peanut butter and jelly cracker sandwich and popped it into my mouth. Then I sent another one in there to join it. Together they were awfully noisy.

"Now you are being childish," she said.

She may have had a point. I may not have cared. I popped another cracker.

Fran simply slapped the phone down on some hard surface, and Mary picked it up.

"Keir," Mary said immediately, in her gruff Mary tone. "Are you being an immature jerk about this? Just tell me, because if you are, then I win five dollars, because I bet Fran you would do this and she insisted you wouldn't."

That would be about right. That would be how it

would go. Fran would bet on me, while Mary would bet against. Fran would be hopeful while Mary would be dubious.

Fran would be wrong, while Mary would be right.

"I am not," I said, trying to repay Fran for her perverse misguided loyalty to me. "Put Fran back on, would you, Mary?"

"Can't. She's gone. Listen, Keir. We want to be there for your graduation. You know that. You cannot deny that. You know we are dying to see you and Dad."

"So, why Wales?"

There was a pause. Unlike Fran, Mary had no problems with pausing.

"You're unbelievable, do you know that? Really, Keir. Wales is Wales. Wales is a wonderful opportunity, socially, educationally, geographically, all that. It is not a reflection on you or Dad. You have to stop seeing things that way. We love you. Got that, goofus? We love you, to bits and pieces. Dad, too. But you'll see, when you're out, when you're here. You'll see."

"What am I going to see, Mary?"

"Are you eating crackers? Are you eating Ritz sandwiches? God . . . Fran, did you know Dad had him on the tranquilizer crackers for this?" she called.

Fran was back on the line. I was back to being silent.

"Come on, Keir," she said softly. "Don't do this. I feel bad enough. Please?"

"You all set up there?" Dad called from downstairs. "Need any more . . ."

Suddenly I got it. It had to be.

"You're pulling my chain," I said happily.

"Oh, Keir—"

"You'll be here."

"Keir, we won't. We can't. You know you're going to have a fantastic time anyway. Wouldn't even notice—"

"You'll be here," I said again. "You wouldn't dare. You're just messing with me, I know it. You'll be here."

"Please—" she said once more.

"Ray," I called, depositing the receiver on my empty plate on the telephone table. "Fran wants to talk to you."

Gigi Boudakian lies facedown on the rug on the bed. There's a strange throw on there, a deep red swirly Turkish type of design, the kind like the carpets her dad would sell, that she will probably also sell eventually when the business is hers if she wants it. It's even possible that throw came from her dad's very shop, handled by her dad's very hands. Gigi Boudakian has her face pressed so hard into that thin foam mattress I am afraid she is going to break her nose on the wood platform beneath.

I can see, without even getting all that close, the bits of fiber and the swirly pattern of the throw's woolly design lying like tiny crop circles on the perfect surface of Gigi Boudakian's perfect face. I have to be able to see it without getting close because she won't let me get close. Which is a shame. A crime and a shame. That is the only crime here, and I desperately need to get her to understand that.

"Listen, please, will you listen to me? You're not listening to me."

That doesn't help anybody, her refusing to listen to me and refusing to speak. I hate it when people I love refuse to speak to me.

"Speak," I say to her. But she is not listening to me.

She goes to the window, turning her back to me and staring away off to nowhere. I don't like the way she is now, all brooding and silent, hugging herself. She worries me.

She bears no resemblance to any version of herself I have ever seen, and that is the saddest statement I can think of.

Slowly and in complete silence I creep up to her at the window. I don't think she can hear me. There are my bare feet, and my carefulness, so I think I am safe, coming up behind her.

I am just behind her, to where I can just about breathe on her, when she moves. She quickly reaches out and grabs the bottom level of the window sash and throws the window open.

Quick as a snake I reach out and around her and seize the window frame and Gigi Boudakian at the same time. I slam the window back down and I wrap her up firmly, pulling her away from the window.

"What are you doing?" I say nervously, angrily. "We're three floors up—you want to get killed? What are you doing?"

She's still not talking. I have her wrapped up snugly, her arms pinned to her sides, my nose right in her ear, smelling her skin, her hair. For a second I cannot hold my eyes open, the way you can't when you sneeze. Only it is the overwhelming sense of Gigi, and of what I feel for Gigi, that has my eyes shut.

How can things go so wrong? How can people be so wrong?

"You have to talk to me, Gigi. If people don't talk to each other, then they get everything wrong. You have got everything wrong."

She is breathing a little faster, but still there are no words coming. I can feel her heartbeat, through her back, into my chest. That makes my own heart kick in triple-time with I don't know what of a feeling, but it is a massive feeling. It's a lot of feelings, and they are all massive, and they are fighting one another and they are killing me.

"You hurt *me*, you know, Gigi. That's right. You're the one who punched me and scratched me, and I would never, ever even think of doing anything like that to you. You don't have to be afraid of me, because I have never hurt you and I would never hurt you, and I'm not even keeping you here so that whole window thing was just crazy."

I feel a slight shifting of her position in my arms, and I have to respond by squeezing her just a little bit tighter. I don't want to restrict her. But she has to understand. She has to hear me out and talk to me and work this out before we can go anywhere, and I know we can do it. And, I have to say, the harder I squeeze Gigi Boudakian, feel her bones and smell her skin, the more helplessly I love her and the less I want to let her go.

"Please speak to me," I whisper into her ear, squeezing her. "Please speak to me."

But all she does is make a whimpering noise.

The graduation ceremony was exactly as boring and stiff as it was supposed to be. I was on the brink of nodding off at almost every moment. Once, emerging from a pleasant mini nap, I almost walked out, flashing back, thinking I was sitting sweating out a graduation from the past, a graduation I didn't actually have to be at, so why bother. I did that at Mary's sweaty boring graduation, and again at Fran's sweaty boring graduation. I walked out. But I came back, too. I was clapping for them at the end, just as hard as anybody there was clapping for theirs.

Fran and Mary weren't walking out on mine, though, and they weren't clapping that I could hear. They'd made good on their threat not to come.

I was there for them. Just as I always had been and always would be there for them. Their absence was inexcusable.

But I had Ray. Like they had Ray. Like my mother had Ray and still has him, dead as she is, like everybody has Ray. That's loyalty right there. That's the way your people should be, through thick and thin, if life is going to mean anything at all.

"Thanks, Dad," I said as we headed to the car after the ceremony.

He was crying a little bit. We tended to talk less, when Ray was crying. We tended, actually, to talk about not much more than his crying.

"Could you stop that, now?"

"Leave me alone."

"Thanks, though. Anyway. Thanks, Dad. Ya big baby."

"What, thanks?"

"You know what for. You want me to drive home?"

"I can drive. Why wouldn't I drive? I'm still the father here, y'know."

"Here, let me drive. You're scaring me. Like when Father Murphy died."

Oh, no. Father Murphy, his dog. I said it. I didn't mean to. Big mistake.

"Aw. Remember ol' Murph?"

He still never knew I hated ol' Murph. He still refused to acknowledge that his dog and I didn't get along. Was that a bad thing or a beautiful thing? I don't know, but it made me want to give the old man a squeeze, except that might make him more wobbly still.

"There, you drive," he choked, dangling the keys.

Emotional guy, my dad.

We pulled out of the parking lot. We got waves from all over. From lifelong friends, from new friends, from guys I'd be pressed to even name. Call me. I'll call you. You coming by later? Don't blow me off. I wouldn't blow you off. I'm surely blowing him off. Ray kind of slumped in his seat while I spirited him out of there, like some big-timer trying to dodge the paparazzi on the way out of his court appearance.

"Thanks," I said, "for, like, raising me and all that. You know. Remember? All that stuff you did."

He sniffed. "Oh right," he said, "that."

We drove the rest of the way home in silence, the two of us just appreciating the lovely warm afternoon through familiar streets, windows wide, radio playing low from Ray's old jazz station.

It was altogether too somber when we pulled into the driveway and walked, still so silent, up the walk to the house like we had done fifty million times before, but that felt like we would never ever, not even once do again. I knew this was not entirely rational, but it was the feeling all the same. Everything right now had the feeling of lasts, of finishes, of playing out for good, forever. We would do these things again, me and my dad, surely. Surely we would, another fifty million times, just like this, and fifty million more in other ways. Nothing was finishing, nothing had to finish if we didn't say so, no matter how it felt right now.

I did something then that I hadn't done since I was a small somebody else. I took Ray's hand, reached out and took it as it swung there, as he ambled up the stone path in front of me.

And he took mine, without looking, without commenting, without even seeming to notice. His fingers curled tight around mine and held on.

"Risk?" he said as we came into the living room.

We had an hour before Rollo was supposed to pick me up.

"Indubitably," I said. A word I picked up early, and used to sound light and sparky when I needed.

"Refreshment?" I said.

"Indubitably," he said.

We sat down to two icy cold Heinekens and a large bag of Bugles, across the globe from each other, to settle the events of world conflict and control.

But first we did the natural thing: Each capped the fingertips of one hand with Bugles, held them up for show, then ate them off one by one before getting down to serious military business.

We had, in the past months, each been guilty of blatantly pathetic strategy when necessary, in order to keep this one continuous game alive and balanced. But now time thundered on. We seemed to have just sat down. We seemed to have just started. We seemed to have plenty more time and turns still in front of us when Dad glanced at his watch and reminded me that Rollo would be here any minute now.

"What do you want to do?" he asked.

We hunched over the board, staring and studying, more like chess than silly old Risk, more like a fresh and interesting compelling new contest than the same peanut we had been nosing back and forth across the table at each other since the day Fran left the house.

What do I want to do?

"About what?" I asked.

"About the game, of course."

I pondered.

"Keep playing?" I suggested.

"You sure?"

"I don't know."

"Maybe somebody ought to win," he said.

"You think?"

"Well, no. Not necessarily. But I thought maybe you thought . . ."

"No. Not really."

Rollo pulled up outside, with his usual fuss. He beeped his horn. The car had many horns, which Rollo changed like people change cell phone ring tones. This one played "Pomp and Circumstance."

The two of us got up from the table and went to the door to greet Rollo.

"Hey," Rollo said as soon as the door opened.

"Hey," I said.

"Hey," Dad said.

"Ray," Rollo said. "You going to get all weepy here? You haven't been getting all weepy like you do, spoiling the kid's day, have you?"

"Nah, he hasn't," I said.

"Yes, I have," Ray said, all solemn and repentant like a schoolboy.

"Well, cut it out. This is a joyous occasion, one of the finest times in a boy's life, maybe the best time he'll ever have what with everything that's waiting for him out there in the world, and you shouldn't be raining on his damn parade. So grow up, ya big fat baby."

"All right, all right," Ray said.

I turned to face him, to shake his hand before leaving. "Rain if you want, Ray," I said, then, pulling him close and hugging his soap-smelling neck, added, "but I do wish you wouldn't."

He hugged me back, then pushed me away. "Got a minute?" he asked.

"Meter's running," Rollo said, and we all knew he meant it.

"Shut up, Rollo," Dad said, and shut the door, leaving him standing on the step.

He went to the hall closet and brought out a box, neatly wrapped in luminous green foil paper. His packages were always wrapped perfectly, in the nicest papers, like he had taken some wrapping course someplace.

"What is this, Ray?" I said, looking it over as if I could tell anything from the paper.

"It's your present," he said.

"What are you doing? Rollo is my present, remember? And he's not a cheap present either."

"I know," he said, motioning for me to shut up and open it.

I tore it open like I always did, carefully, so he could reuse the paper. He had a wrapping-paper graveyard in a corner of the basement for reusables that he nurtured like a bonsai garden. Though I never saw him reuse any.

"It's a phone," Ray said, in case I couldn't tell.

It was a good present. I had been planning to get a new cell. Mine was a bit old, out of date, simple and large, but I hadn't replaced it because I found I hadn't been using it. This one was very nice.

"It's very nice, Dad," I said.

"It's more than nice," he emphasized. "It's prepaid. Forever. And it'll work anywhere. You go to Saturn, this'll work. You can call and tell me how Saturn is, if it's hot, or whatever."

I felt a big smile crossing my face. "Funny, I was thinking I'd be visiting Saturn . . . maybe today."

"Anytime, anywhere, forever, Keir. Understand? You get it? You—"

I shoved him out of my way as I headed up to my room.

"I get it, ya big dope."

I ran to my room, ran back down.

"Here," I said, shoving my terribly wrapped long box of a gift into his hands.

He looked at it. "You're a terrible wrapper," he said.

"Is that important?"

"Did I teach you to wrap like that? I don't think so."

"Open it."

"Why are you giving—"

"Seemed appropriate. Just open the damn thing."

Rollo's horn blew. "Jumpin' Jack Flash."

Ray opened his package to find a bottle of his favorite Scotch whiskey, Laphroaig.

"I know, not much of a surprise," I said.

"It's the thought," Ray said. "And a tasty thought it was."

He ripped it right open, took a long pull. Grimaced. Sighed. Passed the bottle to me, and I followed suit, replacing the sigh with a wheezy groan.

"Love ya, Ray."

"Love ya, Keir."

And I was off. I had my new anytime anywhere gift tucked securely under my arm. Ray had his likewise.

Rollo's limo was all the best of life, on wheels. There were two televisions inside, and a stereo with enough wattage to shoot me through the back window if I cranked the volume up all the way. There were two couches, burgundy velour, running up alongside either side of the backseat. And there was a bar, a full wet bar, complete with fridge and sink and ice and little wedges of lime, and onions and olives and a mini blender and cans of crushed fruit and a basket of uncrushed fresh fruit for mauling in the blender to make any kind of exotic drink you wanted.

It was all the best of life, on wheels.

And it was my plan to make the best of the best of life while I had it. I was going to be silly and drive through the drive-through just for a snack. I was going to drive up and down the main streets and the quiet streets just showing off. I was even going to make Rollo go down Byner Street, which is a dead end and too narrow, just to make him have to U-turn and have all the neighbors gawk that much longer. All the while I was going to keep the smoked windows up, the air-conditioning humming, the music honking, and the bar open.

I was going to do all that. But I didn't.

I did something else.

"You know where I've always wanted to visit, that I have always heard about but never got to visit?" I shouted to Rollo.

He rolled down the glass partition between us. "Say the word," he said.

"The middle of nowhere. You know how people are always saying they were in the middle of nowhere? Well it sounds cool to me, and I would really like to have a look."

Rollo said nothing for a few seconds, just kept driving straight up the main road out of town. Then, "Don't think I could locate it, Keir."

"Then we could get lost on the *way* to the middle of nowhere. Nobody's ever done that before."

Again he paused. "Ah, yeah," he said. "Any other ideas?"

Look at me there. Look at me. Conditions could not have been better. I had the damn world on a plate. I had paradise on wheels on this, my high school graduation day. No limits, no curfews, no cares about where or when or how to get my jollies or how much it was going to cost or who was going to tell me no, because nobody was. Ray wasn't going to, and Rollo wasn't going to, and the only people who might even raise an eyebrow were my sisters, and as we all knew my sisters weren't coming, goddamn it. So no girls, nobody says no.

And Rollo wanted to know if I had any ideas.

I was in the very top of conditions at the top of the world on the top day of top days, of course I had ideas.

And I wished they would go away.

That feeling that I had when I told Ray I didn't want a party, that feeling was growing like a tumor in my head now. You know that feeling you have when you are doing something you don't really know how to do, like skiing or sailing or speaking French, and you are panicky about the next move, the next breath? Even, or especially, if it is a thing you have done loads of times, but now you are a stranger to it? Even if you are sort of an expert at whatever it is, and now you are a stranger to it so it scares you even more? That was how I felt, on my graduation day, inside Rollo's ride, pinned between the bar and the couches and the sound system inside, and the whole world on the outside.

I was paralyzed. Certain that whatever move I made was going to be the wrong one. So afraid. How stupid was that? I was so afraid, even though there was nothing to be afraid of, and everything to play for.

I'm lying. I said I wouldn't do that to you, but I am. I knew well what I was afraid of, why I was paralyzed. It was because I didn't know, under the pressure of the day, which part of me was going to show up. The way I didn't know on that night whether I was a football player or a soccer player. Like when I couldn't even tell, watching the tape afterward, whether I was looking at me or not. Like it was a full-blown contest, a game of Risk, for the territory inside me.

So that was the truth of it there, but the truth was frankly a stupid truth. A guy needs not to be afraid of himself. A guy needs to be certain of himself, and sometimes a guy just needs to snap the hell out of it.

I wished one of the linemen from the football team was there to smack me straight.

But they weren't, so I'd have to do it myself. I pulled a diet Sprite out of the fridge.

In my pocket was a lonely blue pill. Couldn't remember where I got it or even how long I'd had it, but I was well aware of it now, and I was well aware what it was supposed to do for me. I fingered the little triangle of enthusiasm in my pocket for a minute, then without much enthusiasm I popped it and chased it with the Sprite. I chose. You can't not choose. Out on the field, right or wrong, you have to choose.

I never even answered Rollo.

"Okay, then," he said, hitting one of the last rotaries out of town and circling back in. "I'll work it out."

And so he did.

He knew the town, knew the score, better than me even, better than probably anybody in town. I didn't have to tell Rollo anything to get him to arrive at the only graduation party that really mattered.

When we pulled up to the curb in front of Quarterback Ken's house, the place was rocking, almost visibly. The whole of the A and B list of the school's social classes were either already inside, or on their way in, or on their way out. I sat there behind the smoked glass, watching, while no one could watch me. They could see my car, see my power, see my cool, while I could stay in shadow. Sweet. I watched the windows of the big white colonial house, watched people filing in and out— mostly in—and I felt the vibration of the full might of the Quarterback Ken sound system rumbling under my feet and rattling the crystal glasses of my own private party bar.

Which I wasn't touching.

In a way, what I was doing here was just right. Because if I wanted to show off for everybody, this was as show-offy as I could get. Outside the town's best party, inside the town's best ride. I was welcome to join everyone who was anyone. I was choosing not to. How cool was that?

Not. At. All. I wasn't choosing jack. I was frozen to my plush seat, with my hands frozen in my sad little lap.

You can't not choose.

There was nothing at that party to be afraid of. The only thing that party was missing was me. There was absolutely nothing at that party to be afraid of. The only only thing that party was missing was me.

I sat there staring like a numbskull, like a pervert, until I was shocked right out of the seat and onto my knees by the foreign bleeping sound in my pocket. It was my new phone. It was set way too loud, and the ring tone was "The Battle Hymn of the Republic."

"Jesus," I said into the phone.

"No. It's me." Ray.

"What are you doing?"

"Huh? Nothing."

"Are you drunk, Ray?"

He didn't answer. Then, "Quasi. How 'bout you?"

"Not at all."

"Too busy, are you?"

"No, actually, Ray . . . Dad . . . Actually, I don't know what to do with myself. I'm kind of scared, Dad. All of a sudden. Like a panic. And I don't know why."

It took Ray a long silent while to get his head around that. At the same time I realized I was still down on my knees talking to him.

"Maybe you're just emotional," he said finally. "Maybe it's just all catching up with you now. About graduating, and moving on, and about all you're leaving behind. Maybe that's it."

He was no shrink, my dad. Nobody would tell you that. But I felt better. A little tiny bit better, just from talking to him and listening to his quasi-drunk view of me. I got off my knees and onto the seat and flopped back.

"Think so?" I asked.

"Sure," he said. I could hear him swig from his Laphroaig.

"You drinking out of the bottle, old man?"

"You stop worrying about me and go have yourself a good time."

"I don't know—" I started, but was interrupted by a knocking at the window. "Dad," I said, "I have to go. There's somebody here for me."

"Somebody there for you. A girl somebody?"

"Ya, Dad. I gotta go. Thanks. I love ya. Drink out of a glass."

"Have the time of your life, son. I love ya. I'll drink any damn way I please."

I could feel my mood instantly elevate as the electric window descended. "Hiya, Gigi," I said.

"Happy graduation," Gigi Boudakian said, leaning in the window. And she kissed me.

It was a wonderful thing, a soft, heather honey kiss, just *here* enough so it felt like it wasn't charity, and like I wasn't her brother, but just *there* enough so I didn't think it was more than it was. Amazing skill, that kind of communication, and I didn't imagine a guy could ever manage it.

"Same to you," I said. Followed too quickly by, "Did your boyfriend come home for the graduation?"

She laughed in a friendly way. "No," she said.

My whole head heated up with the sparks of all the wrong romantic ideas.

"He'll be here tonight, though," she said, poking me in the arm.

"Oh, good," I lied. "Would you like to come in for a drink? We have those little bottles of champagne that girls like."

"In the spirit of the day, I will ignore the remark and accept the offer."

And she accepted the little champagne. I accepted my own offer of a tumbler full of ice and Jack Daniels.

"So what were you going to do," Gigi Boudakian asked over quietly thumping background music, "just sit outside and watch like a chauffeur-driven stalker?"

"No," I said, looking down at the rug between my feet, blushing. "No, of course not." I wasn't completely sure if she was wrong. I wasn't sure if the watching I was doing and the watching a stalker would be doing were entirely different things, but I was prepared to give myself the benefit of the doubt. "I was going to come in. I was just talking to my dad for a minute."

I showed her my phone. "He gave me this," I said anxiously. "For my graduation, my dad gave me this. Prepaid, like, for life. Nice, huh? Nice phone. I thought I should call him on it, try it out. He's home, all by himself. Then he went and called me first. So I was talking to him. He misses me, I think."

Gigi Boudakian's face broke out in such a megasmile, I couldn't help but smile some myself. That's what a smile from her does to you.

She kissed me again, on the cheek. Just missed my ear.

"You're no killer at all," she said. "You are a big cream puff."

"That's what my dad says," I said.

Gigi had a second mini champagne, and by the time she finished it I had poured my third Jack Daniels, still relying on the remnants of the original ice.

"I think it's time," she said brightly, sort of waving away my glass as she said it.

I drank my shot down very fast.

Gigi Boudakian touched my hand. All senses returned to full power, and shocks like I was grabbing the terminals of a car battery ran up my arms and into my chest. I looked at her. Gigi Boudakian's slender hands there, were the most beautiful, the softest, the warmest. Gigi Boudakian's eyes there, were the softest, warmest, brownest, the feeling spread, my chest filling, overfilling, overflowing, the mad electrical sense rising up into my throat, sinking down into my stomach, down, down, Gigi Boudakian, doing nothing more than touching my hand with her hand. . . .

"You want to go now?" she asked me.

"I want to go now?" I asked me.

She took this for an answer and pulled me from my seat as she opened the car door with her other hand.

Pretty much everyone I had ever known was inside Quarterback Ken's house when we got there. The music was ten thousand times louder than it was in the limo, and more confused, since there were different monster sound systems punching away from at least three different locations in the house.

"Killer!" somebody called out.

"Killeeer," somebody amended.

I waved, kept walking, happy to follow along behind Gigi Boudakian. I wove through throngs, crowds, churning, slapping masses of dancers, slack-limbed roomfuls of rabble, and as we entered each doorway and exited out the other side, I found myself farther and farther away from Gigi, chasing after her vapor trail as she meeted and greeted and veered off into a crowd of lady friends. Then, lost and alone, I stopped.

I was in a room surrounded by food. I did not want any food. The music was good, though. It was the same music I didn't like before. It was great music now. I hated dancing, always did. I liked dancing now. Started, in fact, dancing in place.

Where were the girls? Everywhere, actually. There were girls, as well as guys, everywhere you looked. Everybody said hi.

"Hi."

"Hi."

Everybody was great. Everybody was really great today. Why were there so many people here? There were not this many people in the school. There could not be this many people graduating. Why were so many of these people strangers to me?

"Hi."

"Hi."

But lovely strangers they were. I could dance with any of them.

I started dancing with this tall red-headed girl I had never seen before. Not that I was much of a judge, but I thought she was a great dancer.

"You're a great dancer," I said. Screamed, really.

"No, I'm not," she said, going faster, faster, shooting her impossibly long arms into the air. Everybody in the crowd, as if attached to her by strings like marionettes, stuck their hands in the air.

Wow. These girls were great.

I didn't want these girls, though. They were okay, of course . . . but I wanted . . . other girls. Where was Gigi Boudakian?

And where were my girls? My Mary, my Fran. They would love this.

Where were they? I suddenly blued up.

They should have been here. They should have. Why

weren't they? Did they not care? What was so important about tests? All right, I knew tests were important, but the tests were tomorrow and this was today, and today was supposed to be *my* day. They needed to see me having my day. How could me and my day even really be happening if they weren't there to see it?

The tall red-headed girl was not dancing with me now. She had drifted. She was still in my region, but she seemed more in the orbit of another guy. A real football player, not a kicker. A bastard running back.

I picked up an unguarded lemon vodka drink in a bottle and left the room.

Out in the hallway I ran into Delia, who I dated once with no lasting effects. She was drinking, and weirdly dancing, caught as she was in the crosscurrent of reggae coming up from the basement and the electro nonsense of the room I had just left. She had a crowd moving along with her, guys and girls alike, nobody doing a particularly smooth job of things, nobody standing out as notably awful either. It was like a class of beginners at an aerobics class.

"Killer!" the crowd hollered.

What a rush. Never expected that. Must have been twenty of them, all putting a whole lung into it. I never heard anything quite like it, and I have to admit—have to admit that the sound of that name wasn't sometimes a bad sound at all.

"Yoyoyo," I yelled in return, waving my vodka drink.

"Where is Gigi Boudakian?" I yelled, right up close into Delia's ear.

She pulled away, partly out of my screaming so up close, partly to be coy.

"Killer got a crush," she said, laughing and pushing me playfully.

"Shut up, I don't," I said.

"Shut up, you do," she said, pushing me again.

I felt myself smiling against my will. My will wanted me to be cool and calm, my will wanted me to be stern and secretive. My will wasn't good for anything.

"Ya, I do," I said. "Got a big ol' crush."

Delia squealed, like we were still in sixth grade, talking about this crush business. "I don't know where she is," she said. "I think she went, like, over there," she pointed, "up there," she pointed, both hands pointing now, in slightly different directions. "Her cell went out and she was looking for the phone, I think."

I thanked her and started upstairs.

"You better be careful," she called, "or her boyfriend's gonna shoot you when he gets here."

I turned, walking up backward while talking over the music. "Who's the killer? Who's the killer here?"

I hit the top of the stairs and found her, Gigi Boudakian, trying to make conversation on a telephone, a very old-fashioned telephone, black and shiny and shaped something like a dumbbell. She wasn't having a great deal of success with the phone, but the look on her face said that there was some information coming through.

I waved at her. She looked right through me. I stood right there and refused to be transparent. She stopped ignoring me and stared hard at me. She was scowling at the telephone as if she was trying to intimidate it, and when that did not work she turned on me.

She waved at me, impatiently, aggressively, like a traffic cop. Move along. Nothing to see here.

I moved along, down the upstairs corridor, checking doorways, looking back over my shoulder to see her now gesticulating wildly at whoever was on the phone.

As if I had been expected, as if this was all for me, a door burst open at the far end of the hall, and as I continued staring back longingly, sympathetically, and perhaps obsessively at Gigi Boudakian, I was seized by a cluster of hands and arms and hauled into the room. The door slammed and locked behind me.

"Killer!" Quarterback Ken shouted down into my face as he squeezed me in a headlock.

"Ken!" I shouted back.

"Killer!" he shouted, squeezing a little harder, giving my head a little yank and a twist for emphasis.

"Ken," I said once more, though it came out now as a kind of strangled rasp.

He let me go, straightened me up, and gave me a proper hug. I hugged him back, looking around at the same time.

We were in a big, lush bedroom that had to be his parents'. Surrounding us in a tight, quiet semicircle was the core of the football team.

A weirdly quiet semicircle. These were not shy guys. There were a pair of twins, Cory and Bam (whose real name was Brian), the two starting offensive tackles who spent the last four years protecting Quarterback Ken. They weighed something near six hundred pounds between them, had received offers from, like, six hundred schools between them, and had the kind of personalities that probably come along inevitably with that kind of bulk and good fortune and the knowledge that somebody huge is always there watching your back. That is, they were loud, aggressive, scary, fun, cool, tense, mean, privileged, confident, unpredictable, unsurprising, lazy with bursts of superhuman antisocial energy. And blond. White blond. They looked like a couple of big Swedish farm boys. They filled a room.

Usually.

"Hey guys," I said, letting go of Ken to go shake hands.

"Yo, Keir," Bam said warmly, "good to see you. I was hoping you'd make it."

"Good to see you, Keir," Cory said, offering me a handshake like a fistful of warm rigatoni.

The whole room was like this. Cool. I went around the semicircle of football players as if it were a reception line for the president's birthday party.

"James," I said, nodding at James, our lanky and beautiful wide receiver with the great legs but the hands of stone. James spent the year blazing around the field, looking like a threat, catching very few passes but looking fab doing it.

"Arthur, Phil, Jon-Jon," I said to our pudgy pack of defensive linemen. I realized our players were even good enough to have arranged themselves by position, as if there were some chart someplace that instructed offensive players to hang with offensive players, defensive with defensive, with our fearless leader Quarterback Ken there to stir the ingredients as necessary.

I was special teams. It is just a saying. It is just a term, and a kind of stupid term to boot, in that glorious way only sports can be that stupid. But momentarily, it had meaning for me. I was a kicker, the kicker, neither offense nor defense, untethered, unaligned, unmarked. I could go where I wished, mingle as I wished, do exactly whatever I wished.

Kicker not cornerback. I was never a cornerback, really.

As I stood mutely with my associates and homes of the last few years, the music thudded along the floorboards, up through my shoes and into my bones from all the other places in the house where people were acting like there was a party going on.

"Hey," Ken said as he came up behind me and slipped an arm around my shoulders and squeezed me once more.

But it was a warm squeeze this time, a soft and gentle squeeze.

"Hey," I said back, turning to catch his face right in mine. "No parents, huh?"

He giggled, sort of distractedly, as if somebody in a far corner of the room had said something.

"No," he said, "no parents."

"No parents," James said with a similar giggle, and they all appeared to take this as a cue to disperse. A few guys spread out over the generous expanse of the Quarterback Ken family bed. A couple more went to hang precariously by a wide-open window, while one or two more seemed to merely hug the walls looking for plaster cracks.

Ken started guiding me toward the dresser.

"Ya," he said, his head brushing alongside mine as he nodded, "that's their graduation present to me. They cleared out. I have until Monday, free-range, full amnesty, no questions asked as long as nobody gets injured, nothing gets broken, and no authorities arrive on the premises. Or if any of that does happen, it's covered up by the time they're back."

He was giggling again by the time he had finished speaking and we had reached the highly polished cherry-wood top of the dresser and its great big mirror staring us in the faces.

Quarterback Ken's face had a strange, lopsided, unrecognizable smile, like he had had a stroke but that it wasn't an unpleasant thing. My face, I was shocked to find, looked shocked.

"What is this?" I asked, looking down at the silver tray.

"What do you think it is?" he asked.

"I wouldn't know," I said.

"Oh, I think maybe you would know."

"I think I don't."

"Would you like to know?"

"Well, Ken, that's why I asked in the first place. To know."

"No, no," he said, dramatically undraping his arm from me so he could bend low and address the tray.

He picked up the short green plastic straw and inhaled a straight white stripe.

When he stood back up again and tried a smile on me, the live half of his face had sunk to meet the floppy half.

"But that doesn't tell me what it is," I said.

"It's whatever you want," he said, pointing like a general over a battlefield map. "You want to go up, you stick to this area over here. You want to go down, then these here are what you're looking for. Then, of course, we have whatever combination of the two you might be interested in."

I took a half step back. "Are you pulling my leg?"

"If that's what you want," he said, reaching down toward my leg. My kicking leg.

I grabbed him by the shoulders and brought him back up. "Really, Ken," I said. "All this stuff . . . serious stuff?"

"Serious as it gets," he said proudly.

I shook my head. "That's, um, that's beyond me, I think, Ken. That's . . . you have to be, like, a freak to be doing that stuff."

"Nah, nah, nah, nah," he said. "You're talking about injecting. This isn't like that. This is just for laughs. Strictly recreational . . . although *seriously* recreational."

As if we had settled something there, he nodded at me, patted my cheek a couple of times, then went at the silver tray again, this time taking one from column A, one from B. The Swedish farmers, cashing in, I supposed, on years of faithful service protecting the quarterback's body, were now edging up to collect on the debt.

Ken stepped aside to let them in.

"Your choice," he said, glassy-eyed, his speech slowing as he tried to blink away the wet eyes and twitchy nose.

It might be understating things to say that I was no choirboy. Truth is, I had no aversion to the occasional stimulant. Probably that was the issue, that maybe I'd have been better off with some kind of aversion. Not that I was inclined to go mental on cocaine or whatever. Just that . . . it tended to keep me *going*, beyond the point when I should have been finished. It was like being kept in the game long after you should be taken out and so you spoil it for everyone.

I thought about mistakes I had made in the past. I thought about when things went wrong. And I realized it was never an issue of *intent*, but of *intensity*. I was a good guy, recall. I could do things and be okay. I could join in and have fun and not cause problems. I didn't have to be afraid of any of this stuff. I didn't have to lock myself away from the action, as long as the action didn't get too hot.

"Right, just a line, then," I said, stepping up. "But mix it, one from column A and one from column B together. To balance me out."

"Ah, a very sensible guy," Ken said, and right away did the required scooping and mixing.

Without fuss I bent into it, and it bent into me. I straightened up, shook my head like a horse. My head filled and sped up. Eyes went wide, all went bright. My heart raced and mellowed parallel, like I had two partner hearts working together, and only just now they were broken open and shown to me.

I had two whole hearts. How could I have missed that? Lucky me.

I saw my reflection in the mirror, overexcited and overcharged, and I backed away.

"Now you'll have another," Ken said with a big grin.

"Now I won't," I said, hands out in front of me. "I think . . . maybe I'll just go and find a drink. If that's okay. You know, I wasn't really planning on staying, so I'm sorry I didn't bring anything . . ."

"Hey, shut up," he snapped, as if the strain of keeping his eyes clear was infuriating him and I was somehow responsible for it.

I was about to apologize again, when I realized I had it wrong.

"Bozo," he said. "Killer, Bozo. Don't you dare apologize. You don't bring drink here." He started slapping himself on the chest. "I provide, for my friends. You're my friend. Everything is on the house here. Here . . ." He reached into his pants pockets and came up with something cupped in his hand. He took me by the wrist and with a little flicking gesture ejected all the contents of his hand into my open palm, like an old-timer giving pocket change to a little kid.

They were pills, a few like the blue triangle one I scarfed earlier, a few gel capsules, a few that looked like aspirin.

"I don't want these," I said. "Ken, this is too much. This is your stuff. You keep it, don't go wasting it—"

"I'm not *wasting* anything," he said. "I got millions. Anything you want. What do you want?"

"Really, nothing," I said, and then took a harder look at the contents of my palm. Hmm. The pill from earlier . . . I was, in fact, feeling awfully better. Awfully warm. Awfully . . . *nice*. Awfully fearless and in control.

"Maybe just this one," I said. "Maybe—"

"Maybe nothing," he said, grabbing my fist and curling it up into a ball so I couldn't refuse any of it. "If you don't just shut up, and take my gift, and be a good party guest . . ." Here he either lost his train of thought or was actually thinking about what he would have to do if

I didn't be a good party guest. ". . . then we're all going to kick your ass. And then drop you out that window." He looked quite pleased with his solution. "Aren't we, guys?" he called out, to general murmuring and gurgled support from the team.

I looked at the pills. I looked at Quarterback Ken. I looked at the open window. I shoved the pills into my pocket.

"Happy graduation," Ken said.

"Thanks," I said.

He hugged me. "I love you, man."

"Well no, really you don't," I said, hugging along.

"Ah, you're probably right," he said, spun, and went back to the silver tray, where scholar athletes were now gathering like big cats around a carcass.

"I'll just go get a drink then," I said.

Nobody objected. I left.

When I stepped back out into the hallway on the second floor of the Quarterback Ken residence, my senses were swarmed, inside, outside. Everything seemed brighter, like a floodlit movie set. The music was enormous, filling my body and rattling it, from the bottom up. My stomach was filled with I didn't know what, but whatever it was I had swallowed it whole and it was dancing. And here is a thing: I flashed on my sisters. Not like that, not like a freak. But I couldn't believe they were not here. I couldn't believe this day was here and they were not.

I had never had a day, I mean, you know, a *day* in my life without them. I missed the hell out of them. I was so goddamn mad at them. They knew how important they were. They knew, Mary and Fran.

Your family should be there. Your family should always be there. What does it say about you if they aren't? It's inexcusable.

Then my eyes came to rest on Gigi Boudakian, still at the telephone table.

Only, "rest" would not be the correct word. They were not resting, my eyes, when they were on Gigi Boudakian. She glowed, in my eyes, above and apart from everything around her. She was powered from within, wattage firing up from her while the rest of the hallway, the rest of the world, went completely flat.

I was so stunned, I was so jumpy inside, I was so much running on pure feelings now rather than my own thinking power, that I nearly failed to notice that Gigi Boudakian was not in a party spirit as I stood there shamelessly staring at her. I nearly failed to notice that Gigi Boudakian was in tears.

Her full bottom lip puffed out and pulled back, puffed out, pulled back as she talked to whomever she was talking to on the phone. Then it puffed out, remarkably, pneumatically, dramatically, as she sat in unhappy silence listening to the words of whatever monster could possibly speak words to make Gigi Boudakian cry. I watched, I suppose, the way people watch sports on TV, moving, twitching, shifting along with the action as my body language attempted to influence the outcome of whatever was going on there in that phone conversation.

I was doing the lip thing as I watched her doing the lip thing, puffing it out, pulling it back, puffing it out, and then biting it to stay in place and show Gigi Boudakian to be happy now and not, and not, and not anywhere near tears.

"What are you *doing*?" Gigi Boudakian yelled at me as she placed the phone receiver in her lap and glowered.

What was wrong? It wasn't me. It wasn't me making Gigi Boudakian cry. It would never be me making Gigi Boudakian cry, it was me standing here rooting for her, rooting for her lip and for happiness and rooting for whoever it was to say the right thing and do the right thing, whatever the right thing was that would put Gigi Boudakian's face back the way it should always be. Even if that right thing for her and for him was not the right thing for me. Even if that.

"Do you *mind*, Keir?" she said to me. "Go downstairs. Or go back in there with the secret society."

For lack of any other ideas, I treated this as an actual conversation. "No," I said, nodding back toward the bedroom door. "That's not my kind of—"

"Go!" she snapped, with a small shriek that could not ever have come out of Gigi Boudakian.

I walked down the hall, passing by her with a dumb little mumbled "Sorry," and took the stairs.

"And could you bring me a drink, please, Keir?" she said in a whole different voice, sad and tired and something apologetic all at once.

I went directly to the food and drinks center and realized quite clearly the minute I got there that I really wanted neither food nor drink. But I found the lemon vodka drinks that Gigi Boudakian wanted, and I got two of them.

Like a good boy, like a very good boy, I returned directly with both drinks. Like we were somehow having a drink together, Gigi Boudakian and the phone and myself. I stood there. I could have been waiting for a tip.

"Ke-ir," she said, exasperated, saying my name with two syllables.

She did not need to say more. I saw her lip quavering again, I saw the effort, I saw the time that was passing over this phone conversation, and I saw I had better go before I saw more than I wanted to see. Good or bad, I had the feeling the outcome would not be something I would like to watch.

Once more downstairs. Once more in this room and that. Once more—no, twelve times more.

And in every room I found what I didn't want. I didn't want any food and I didn't want any drink, and I didn't want any party.

I wanted other people. Not any other people, but *my* people. I don't know where or how I had lost my ability to really enjoy hanging around with the general population, but I had well and truly lost it. It was like I couldn't bear to be very long with people other than the people I loved, and the people I loved were a very compact list and all the rest just made me tense and awkward and angry after the first twenty minutes.

I wanted to go.

The party had become one of those parties. Only more. It seemed perfectly okay with everybody that I just bee-lined out as arbitrarily as I had come in.

I found Rollo asleep, or intensely reading the paper draped over his face. I didn't even bother to wake him as I slipped back into my private spot in the backseat, thinking about what to do, what not to do.

A whole huge part of me wanted just to go home. I could do that, just go back to the house, go quietly to my room, put on music and whack myself to oblivion. That would be good. That would work. It always did, always made me feel mellow and harmless and right.

What I am afraid of now, deeply worried about now, is that Gigi Boudakian is going truly crazy. She is not acting right. She is not acting any way I recognize as normal.

"I'm worried," I say to her after one alarming half hour of silence.

"You better be."

"Gigi, why are you taking this out on me? It's Carl who didn't come. It's Carl who's responsible, for getting you all upset and making you cry and making you crazy. I was the one who was here for you. Why can't you understand that? I was the one who was here, Carl was the one who didn't come."

"Well he's coming now. Today Carl is coming, Keir.

And so is my father. So is everybody, coming for you, Keir Sarafian."

This was just crazy. It was all gone so crazy, I couldn't believe it.

wasn't even aware how long I was sitting there, staring out the window like a zombie. Rollo was still sleeping, though.

Gigi emerged from the house and marched straight across the lawn, straight toward the limo, very much like something in a dream. If I were sleeping like Rollo, this would be exactly the dream I'd be having.

There she was at the window. I even tried to preserve her there. Just for a few seconds, a few seconds with her lovely soft sad face framed in the window, mine to keep. She pressed her face to the glass, cupped her hands around her eyes, trying to see in through the smoke.

"Keir," she called loudly, knocking on the window. "Keir, are you in there?"

She must have disturbed Rollo's sleep, because suddenly

my electric window was opening, and he was growling, "For god's sake, you don't keep a quality girl waiting."

"Hi," said Gigi Boudakian, who looked like she had tired and sad panda eyes now, reddish and watery, black drippy makeup pooling and overflowing from shallow hollows above her cheekbones. It was like when the window opened it revealed what was real, dark and unlovely, and I for one was anxious to not see it.

"Hi," I said, and it sounded like a long, slo-mo sentence as it slurped out of me. "You were looking for me?" My stomach did a sudden leap as I said the words, and heard them.

"Yes," she said.

"Excellent. What for?"

She paused, smiled shyly. "I don't know, actually."

"Good enough for me," I said brightly.

"Stop that," she said, laughing, smacking my arm.

I reached out then, pulling the sleeve of my jacket down over my hand, and dabbed at both of her black, streaky pools to clean them up some.

"You okay?" I asked, squinting for the response.

Gigi Boudakian lowered her determinedly lovely chocolate eyes. "Not really," she said.

"I'm sorry," I said.

She nodded graciously. "Buy you a drink?"

I shook my head graciously. "But I could buy you one." I motioned at my mobile bar.

Gigi blinked twice, nodded, and climbed in.

We drank a drink, and then another, and Rollo drove us around, looking for the middle of nowhere. And that suited us just fine.

At least it suited me. I was into Gigi Boudakian. Everything else had become background, bordering on interference. She talked to me, about people we knew, I think, about music, about college, I think, and maybe about families, definitely, about families, about Sarafians and Boudakians and all and I think, yes, I know, she talked about her boyfriend Carl in the air force and his fateful and nasty and stupid decision not to come home for her graduation. I never enjoyed talking with a pretty girl about her boyfriend more than I was enjoying it right there.

I watched, I listened, I smiled. Gigi Boudakian drank, and Gigi Boudakian was not really a drinker, but sometimes there are just those times.

Then she nearly ruined everything by asking to borrow my new phone.

"I have to try," she said, before stepping just outside the car. "A person has to try, Keir, that's what I think. So I have to try at least one more time."

"I guess," I said, not believing at the moment that a person did, necessarily.

While I waited in the ether of the presence of Gigi Boudakian, I thought it might be a good time for a charm-bravery-confidence booster. I reached a hand into my pocket, fished around, took out a couple of pills. There were a couple of triangles left, and the others, and I thought I would be conservative for now and stick with the tried and true. I gagged one, washed it down, stood there numb and waiting and hoping like hell that my old friend Carl was going to continue to be the most foolish young man in our entire armed services and *not* come to Gigi Boudakian on her graduation day.

Until, just minutes later, I set eyes again on Gigi's eyes, on her so sad red drippy eyes, and right there I repented, reversed, and wished so badly that whatever bad wishing I had done did not contribute to making this so. Because I would even rather have seen him come swooping down out of the sky with a chest full of medals and sweep her away from me than see what I was seeing.

"I'm sorry, Gigi," I said as she sat back in the car, sniffing, wiping with a messy sweep of her elegant hand, then sniffing some more.

"He's not even there now," she said, voice quavering with rage and sadness. "He said he had to stay right there on base, and now he's not even there."

She leaned right up to me, right up close, close enough so I could feel heat coming off her skin, off her flushed face.

"My sisters didn't come either," I said.

"Yes, I know. You told me."

"Did I?" I said.

She giggled. She was sad and sad-faced, but she could giggle too. She could do it all, Gigi Boudakian.

"You are a good guy, aren't you, Keir?"

I examined the statement for any hidden message. Didn't find any.

"I am. I am a good guy, Gigi."

"Why do guys find it so hard to be good guys?"

I shrugged. "I don't. Only sometimes."

She giggled sadly again.

I took her hand, and she let me do it. It was wet. I did not care at all. Even better, in fact. Even nicer. There was more Gigi Boudakian in a wet hand than a dry one and more Gigi was an indisputably good thing.

One tear escaped, then another, running down that beautiful face, spoiling it, ruining everything. I took my free hand—the free hand because the other hand was not letting go, not on your life—and I daubed her high glorious cheekbones with the heel of the sleeve of my jacket once more. And then I reached into my back pocket for my wallet.

"Want to see my mom?" I asked Gigi Boudakian.

I had never before said that, or anything like that, in my life. Not once to anyone.

"I would like that very much," she said, a smile coming through like sunshine burning away a fog.

I handed over the photo I carried, an inferior copy of Ray's piano-top picture.

"Also, that's what my sister Fran looks like. Pretty much. She was supposed to be here too, Fran was. And Mary, too. They were supposed to come."

"I know. You said."

"People are like that, though," I said. "People are just like that. What are you going to do? You ready for another drink?"

"I'm okay for now," she said.

"Don't you hate it when people you love let you down?" I said.

"Yes, I do," she said.

"I hate it when people I love let me down. It's like, the worst thing there is."

"It is."

It is.

Heaven on wheels. I may have thought Rollo's car and all that went with it was the ultimate before, but I had no idea what heaven was then. When Gigi Boudakian heard my idea and didn't so much as blink, when she shouted "Why the hell not!" I told the driver to drive and he said, "Yessir," then I knew heaven and heaven knew me.

Even Rollo couldn't believe it, and Rollo had seen everything.

"What?" he said. "Where?"

"Take us to Norfolk, my good man."

"Norfolk," he repeated. "As in, the college."

"Yup," I said. "Me and my lady friend here are on a mission. To show my sad sisters just a little bit of what they missed."

"You are serious."

"I am serious."

"Young lady, that's okay with you?"

"That is okay with me," Gigi Boudakian said in a sing-song to melt even Rollo's cold, cold heart.

I knew, okay. I knew, what we had here was Gigi's anger at somebody else more than it was her affection for me. But I also knew that I didn't care, and that whatever her level of affection for me I was grateful for it and wouldn't be letting go until it was pried out of my hands. Gigi Boudakian liked me and trusted me enough to make this possible, and right now I was the only guy in the world who could say that. Which, by my definition, made me the finest and luckiest guy in the world for at least some small time.

"Okay," Rollo said, "but you know this is three hours—"

"And one state line," I added.

"I know," Gigi said, and nestled down deep in the upholstery. "I don't have any other plans or obligations. And a nice ride through the country, with my very nice gentleman friend, sounds like a better idea than any other right now."

She was doing it again, mixing sweetness and sadness in the same foggy dew.

"We have loads of drinks and snacks," I said hopefully. "You want a drink and a snack?"

She patted my leg. "Maybe later, thanks." She scootched up closer to me, wedged herself against me, and let all her weight rest on me. She didn't object when I raised my arm up and draped it down over her shoulders.

Heaven on wheels. Nirvana, Valhalla, whatever, this was as close to it as I was ever going to get.

Until *bleep-bleep-bleep* went the rotten little electronic birdcall of a cell phone. Shot through me like electroshock when Gigi bounced up in her seat, pulled my phone out of her bag where she'd forgotten it, and started staring at it.

"What?" I said.

He had returned her call, sort of. She showed me the text message from Carl. HEARD YOU CALLED. WHAT UP?

"He doesn't even have the guts to phone me properly," she said. Then she growled and turned the phone off with that exaggerated aggressive maneuver that doesn't really shut the thing off more thoroughly, but does bend your thumb painfully backward.

"Grrr," she growled again, and I was getting to really like that sound. Then she popped right up, went to the refrigerator, and stuffed the phone inside before slamming the door shut again.

It was my new gift phone she was abusing, but I had no interest in objecting.

"Who needs 'em," I said triumphantly as I grabbed a beer and waved at the phone.

"Who needs 'em," she said lowly, slowly, and sadly.

She leaned up and against and into me once more. I draped my arm over her once more. I tipped my head to one side, onto Gigi's head like a pillow, and I breathed her in. Carl, I thought, was a person who made no sense to me whatsoever.

Gigi fell asleep almost as soon as we left town, and she snoozed off and on for much of the ride. Me, I was right there, awake, alive, alert, but held in place between Gigi Boudakian on the one hand and a beer in the other. I was frozen there, and could not have been more content to be that way. I didn't even open the beer for the first hour, as I alternated between staring out the window at the scenery and staring to see that Gigi was still actually under my arm and I was still actually on this earth.

It seemed like no time and no space had passed when Rollo maneuvered the limo through the twisting roadways of the campus to finally stop in front of the girls' dormitory building. It was an ugly thing, very square and made up of red and white stone blocks and lots of windows that should have made things brighter but made them somehow danker—but the sight of it filled me with a kind of Christmas morning light.

"Gigi," I said to her as Rollo came around to open our door. "Gigi, wake up, we're here."

She stirred slowly, raised herself up slowly, and it was then that I realized how completely numb and dead my arm had gone. I hadn't moved it from that spot around and behind her for three hours. And it would have taken a gunfight for anybody but Gigi to get me to move it still.

As it was, I couldn't exactly move it anyway. I let it sort of fall off the back of the seat and hauled it up out of the car behind me.

"Wow," Gigi said, stepping out into the moonlit evening. "This is a beautiful campus."

She spun around to check it out, and true enough, there wasn't a bad angle on the place. It was a great rolling landscape, laid out with a lot of attention to space. Every building, practically, was set atop its own little hillock, which made for fine views from each one of them, even if it meant a lot of walking for students. The air was so thick with pine you'd be checking your teeth for needles.

"Nice, huh?" I said, puffing up as if I'd built the place myself. "I'm coming here in the fall, you know."

"I know," she said, still gazing off. "I am so jealous."

She was going to a community college in town, so she could still work in the family business.

"You could come and visit me," I chirped. "Like, every weekend."

She poked me in the ribs, which I loved, and I was thinking again, this was the best time and place ever to be. It made me think how much this was like prom night, which was the previous best time and place ever.

"So kids," Rollo said. "What's the plan? Bearing in mind it's another three-hour haul back."

"Well, maybe we won't *go* back," I said, thinking as

soon as I said it what a magnificent and thoughtful thought that was.

"Yes, maybe we just won't," Gigi said, but in a much more frivolous way. She had yet to understand the magnificence of my thought.

"Seriously, though," Rollo said. "I think two hours should be enough for you to visit with your sisters, to interrupt their studies, and to get back home in reasonable time. I got friends in the area, I can go visit and cool my heels and be right back here to meet you. Two hours. Fair?"

"Aren't you coming in, Rollo? Just to say hello?"

Rollo stared at me hard, twisting his head sideways. "What are you talking about? You know your sisters can't stand the sight of me."

"Oh, that is not—"

"Two hours, Keir," Rollo said, ignoring me and walking around to his door. "Have fun, kids."

"This is going to be so cool," I said, standing in the hallway about to knock on the door. "This is going to blow their minds. They never in a million years would have expected me to do this, and they are just going to go mental."

"What kind of mental?" Gigi Boudakian said apprehensively.

"Oh no," I said, "the best kind of mental. Only the best kind." I knocked, seven times. We always did that in our family, the seven-times knock.

We waited. I knocked seven more times.

"All right, I'm coming," came an unfamiliar voice.

The door was opened by a wiry thin girl a couple of years older than me. She was wearing thick red socks for slippers and a pink velour robe. "Can I help you?" she said.

"Ah, I'm looking for my sisters. I'm Keir."

She looked at me blankly.

"Keir. Sarafian. Fran and Mary are my sisters."

"Oh," she said politely, "sorry, I didn't know. I'm Grace. I room with your sisters." She held out her hand and I shook it. So did Gigi.

"I'm Gigi," Gigi said.

"Are the girls here?" I asked, peering kind of impolitely around Grace. I couldn't help it, I was anxious.

"Um," Grace said. "No."

"No?"

"No. Well, not right now. They'll be back, though. Anyway, Fran will, in about an hour. She's out with this really nice Mormon guy, and he always has her back right on time."

I would not have been surprised if you could hear the air escaping from my inflated hopes. Or steam, more like it. *Hisss.*

"And Mary?"

"Mary won't be back until late tomorrow sometime. She went to Baltimore for a couple of days with a few of the other girls. Kind of celebrating the end of exams. Some people finished up on Friday, the lucky ones, so they took off."

As fast as Grace could talk, no, faster than Grace could talk, my body filled with deadness. Starting at my toes and sifting upward, bit by bit, I could feel nothing, until I was simply floating there in the hall outside the door where Mary and Fran were not studying.

I became aware of Gigi Boudakian taking my hand, because I could see it out of the corner of my eye. I couldn't feel it, though, though it was a feeling I would have held onto tight if I could.

"You want to come in and wait?" Grace said. "Like I said, Fran shouldn't be more than an hour, so if you want to wait, you are more than welcome—"

"We'll walk," I said, and started walking just like that. "We'll just go for a walk, Grace, thank you. We'll kill time. It's a nice night, so we'll just do that. Thank you, Grace."

Still floating, still not entirely there, I led Gigi down the hall, down the stairs, out the swinging glass front door. I was still unaware of the fine bones of Gigi's slender hand in my hand. I must have been.

"Ow," she squealed. "Keir, you're hurting me."

She pulled her hand away, and I stopped and stared. "I am so sorry, Gigi. I didn't realize . . ."

"Well, no, I didn't think you realized." She relaxed enough to take my hand again, to take both of them in fact, as she faced me and talked to me. "What are you thinking, Keir?"

"I'm thinking that's probably the worst question in the world. I'm thinking you should never ask anybody that question."

She pulled her hands away from mine, and I was instantly sorry for whatever made her do that. I was quick to grab her hands back again.

"I'm thinking," I said, "that I really, really hate it when people I love let me down."

Why doesn't she hear what I'm saying? Why don't my words say what I am saying?

"I'm sorry. Gigi, I said I'm sorry, remember? I didn't do it."

"Let me out of this room, Keir."

"Why don't you hear me? I'm not keeping you here. I'm just trying to get you to listen to me, and you keep not listening to me."

And she does, too, she keeps right on not listening to me. She keeps saying things that are not true and ignoring important things that are true. We kind of march around the room, circling after each other and away from each other, because I cannot let her near the window, because she is acting like she might do something demented, and I can't let her near the door unless I'm there with her, because she can't be going out there without me. Without the truth. We have to look at the truth and agree on it.

"Can I just try one more time? Huh, Gigi? Okay, there was sex, we had sex, all right?"

Instantly she covers her ears and spins to the floor like a corkscrew. She remains there, clinging to two fistfuls of hair on either side of her head.

"We had sex and okay, it wasn't perfect, but I love you."

It is like blood. Her beautiful liquid chocolate eyes are like spurting blood as she looks up at me now.

"Don't do that," I beg. "Please, Gigi, don't do that to me."

"It wasn't perfect. But you love me," she drones.

She is scaring me. With her tone, her eyes, her presence altogether, she is scaring me. Intimidating me.

"That's right," I say.

"You *raped* me," she says, in that flat, quiet tone that is like an almighty scream.

I close my eyes and I step away from her because I don't know what she is right now, but she is nothing I recognize. She is nothing she is supposed to be.

"Stop with that. That . . . word . . . is so wrong. That word does not belong here. It does not belong in the same room with us. It does not belong in the same *world* with me and you. That word, Gigi, belongs someplace else, with criminals and deviates and psychopaths, but not here, not with us, not with me loving you like you know I do. I did *not*. I could not, ever. You did not say that, Gigi, okay?"

"You raped me."

"What are you *saying*? What are you *doing*, Gigi? This is me, here. This is *me*."

"That's right, Keir. You." She is shaking her head now herself, in disbelief, which is the right thing. Disbelief is the right thing. But she is applying it in the wrong way. When she whispers her next words, I die there on my feet.

"How could you do that to me, Keir? You? Me?"

I shake my head even harder in return, like a dog trying to tear the leg off something. "No, no, no, no. Do you know how far away that is from me? That did not happen. Why are you not listening? I could never make that happen. Especially not to you. Not to *anyone*, but especially not to you. You know that. You *knew* that. Just know it again. Please. Please? Know me again."

"I said *no*."

"You know what happened. You slept with me. Right here. Right there," I rush up toward the bed and point right at it, to catch it before it gets away. "Slept, Gigi. You slept with me, which is even better than sex, which I would trade for the sex a hundred thousand times over."

"I said no," she says with the same dead flatness, the dead flatness that says she is not getting anywhere, not making any progress or even trying.

"I love you. That is what matters."

"I said no. *That* is what matters."

She stares at me as I talk, and for several seconds after.

Her face is all pinched up in a confused rage, and it is breaking my heart for what that confused rage is doing to the fineness of Gigi Boudakian's face, to the fineness of Gigi Boudakian. I am praying inside that this is not permanent, that she is not permanently ruined, and that we can fix this before it all gets out of hand.

How could it get so wrong? How could she not know that I would kill anyone who ever did that to Gigi Boudakian?

After we left Grace, we walked all over the campus of Norfolk U. It was just the right thing to do, to cool down, to think through, to take stock, and it was just the time and place and company to do it with.

Gigi Boudakian was my best friend.

The sky was buckshot with stars, and the pale moonlight guided us wherever we wanted to go. It was almost summer warm, there was just enough of a breeze so you knew the air was there, and Gigi Boudakian held my hand the whole way.

I gave her the tour, the same tour they gave me when I came for my recruiting visit months before. I showed her the neighborhood of clustered dorm buildings, I showed her the stately administration buildings and senior faculty residences that looked more like colonial mansions than school property. I showed her the athletics building where I would be spending so much of my next four years working out on the best equipment with the best physical trainers.

"They have a pool, a beautiful Olympic-size swimming pool, right in there," I said. "You can swim in it with me when you come to visit."

She laughed like she did the other times when I showed her things, and she pulled a couple of my fingers apart.

"Ouch," I said. I was deliriously happy. Couldn't she see that?

"I think if Carl came to a place like this, things would be better," Gigi said, spoiling the moonlight. "I mean, it's closer, it's nicer. In the military . . . he's become more rigid, more . . . macho. Less sweet."

"I'm sweet," I said.

"*You* are, yes. But I don't think the air force has done Carl a lot of good, in terms of us. In terms of men and women and stuff."

"Oh," I said, trying like hell to think of a suitable, supportive-but-not thing to say. "Oh," I said.

"Maybe he'll change. Maybe after tonight, after I'm AWOL for a while and he has to think, maybe—"

"Maybe," I said, suddenly catching a whiff of honey-suckle from somewhere near, somewhere probably within the deep forest of the wildly landscaped science center grounds. I stopped to breathe it. I lifted my nose like a dog on the scent of something he just had to get. Gigi lifted her little fawn nose as well.

"See, it wasn't all bad that your sisters weren't here," Gigi said. Why'd she have to say that? The reminder pulled a few petals off the honeysuckle, pulled my nose down out of the air. "I mean," she went on, "we wouldn't be out here now, and I don't know about you, but this has been the best part of my day."

I sighed. "Ya, mine too."

And it was. This had become our place, this rolling green moonsplashed campus. There was little sign of life outside, and likely not much inside, either. All the sports had finished for the year, and most of the exams. There was enough peace here now to shave off some of the anger and disappointment I was feeling, and enough wide-open imaginative space for me to picture myself here a few months away. Picture myself here and big and happy, a football player in his prime in a prime location. To picture the best of the best possibilities.

"Maybe you could enroll here," I said to Gigi. "I'm going to be a big football player, so I could pull some strings."

I was walking in the opposite direction from the dorms. And I would have happily continued walking, to the edge of the campus, past the edge, out into the broad open fields beyond, and out into whatever was beyond that, clutching Gigi Boudakian's hand the whole way.

But she tugged me now, back toward the dorms. "Thanks, but I already have a college, Keir. And your sister is probably back now, so we should see her."

Half of me changed right there. A full half of me went dark and cold at the change of direction, at the reality of what was back there as opposed to the far better world that was surely out in the direction of the fields.

"Hnn," I grunted, following along passively.

She was standing in the open doorway when we got there.

"Hi," I said coldly.

"Hi," she said warily. "And you must be—"

"Gigi, yes. Hi."

Gigi shook Fran's hand. Nobody shook my hand.

We all went in and sat down on the chunky university furniture that filled Fran's living room area, which was two feet away from the kitchen area. There were three doors that must have led to the bedrooms, all lined up together. The whole place was smaller than the kitchen back home, and it felt monstrously claustrophobic to me. The smell of antiseptic and stale bread hung in the air. I couldn't imagine why someone wouldn't want to get out of there and go home as often as possible. I would.

"So how was graduation?" Fran asked.

"It was lovely," Gigi said. "The sun was shining, the day couldn't have been more perfect."

"Are you not offering drinks?" I asked.

"I don't have any. And judging by the smell of you, I don't think you need any more."

"You don't *have* any? Since when are you—"

"It's okay," Gigi cut in. "Fran's right, we've had enough."

I didn't like that at all. I didn't like Fran for saying it, I didn't like Fran for not having drinks, and mostly I didn't like the way Gigi had to step in there.

I was thinking about saying so when there was a beeping at the window. The first notes of "Start Me Up."

Fran got up and looked. "Oh, god, what is *he* doing here?"

"He's my ride," I said. Had it been that long already? No, couldn't be. "Hold on." I asked Gigi to wait, and I went down to Rollo.

"You're early," I said when I got to his window.

"No, I'm not," he said, tapping his watch. "I am right on time."

"Well, you're early for me. I'm not ready yet."

"Well, you need to be ready yet. Listen, Keir, I've been a sport about this, but now it's time. I have to get back to town."

I stepped back from the car, hands on my hips. I looked up at the stars and around at the still niceness of the quiet campus.

"Okay, go," I said.

"Go?" he said.

"Ya. We're going to stay."

"You are? Really?"

"Ya, why not? We got no classes. We're free. And then Fran can bring us home tomorrow, borrow a car from her friend. That way she can come for a visit, make Ray happy. Sure, there's a plan. You are released."

He looked at me screwy-like. "You serious?"

"I am totally serious. Thanks, Rollo. Thanks for the whole thing. I had a great time."

He shifted the car into gear, shaking his head. "I'm not so sure you did, but okay, kid. Take care."

And he drove off. As I turned away and headed back to the dorms, I looked up and saw both Fran and Gigi looking down at me. I got a jolt. I got shaky. I had to tell Gigi what I did, or anyway, some version of what I did.

I waved and smiled and went back up.

"I told him we needed more time," I said calmly, taking my spot again on the grungy couch next to the girl who made it look warm and inviting. "I told him to give us some more time, so he'll be back again, a little later."

Gigi looked a little uneasy about that, but she didn't object. I gave her my most grateful smile—I was more grateful than she could even know—and turned my attention to my sister.

"Baltimore, Fran?"

Fran let out such a sigh, it was like the central heating wheezing into action. "She has a right to do whatever she wants, Keir. Mary's exams are over, okay? I'm sorry."

"And your exams? Are your exams over too?"

"No, they're not. I have one more, tomorrow afternoon."

I didn't really even have to go to the trouble of objecting to that. We all heard it. I objected anyway.

"Afternoon? You couldn't come to my graduation because you had a test *first thing*, remember? And you were studying all tonight, remember? And so now you are out with a Mormon, and Mary is messing around down in Baltimore, and nobody cares enough to come home to my graduation?"

Fran, who had been leaning forward in her chair, slumped backward. "Remember?" she said. "Do I remember?" She stared at me still, but now with her hands folded in front of her face she was praying. When she spoke, her tone was both hushed and intense. "I cannot believe you are here."

"I just bet you can't. I can't believe *Mary* isn't here. I bet you both never figured I'd check on your lies."

"I cannot believe that you came all the way out here for this. I cannot believe I am looking at you right now. What, because we didn't make it back for graduation? How about if *you* remember. Remember how you walked out of both of *our* graduations?"

"It was really hot. At least I was there."

"You were *there* when it became a blowout party. You were *there* to embarrass us by getting publicly sick *both* times."

A huge hot flush came to my face as I turned to Gigi, who shouldn't have been hearing this.

She smiled. She patted my hand.

She was my best friend.

"I was just a kid."

"You are still just a kid," Fran said. "But that's all right. Sort of. That is who you are. But you have to stop being such a kid at least some of the time, and this is one of those times. I don't want to hurt you, Keir, but . . . okay, the truth is we were not there because we did not want to be there."

"What is wrong with you two?" I barked. "What happened to you?" I turned to Gigi. "We were great. You should have seen us, honest to god. We were the best. You would have wanted to join our family, we were so great together—so close, the best."

I was very sad, listening to myself. Listening to myself talk as if I were talking about a wonderful person who was dead. My stomach climbed up into my chest, and my heart squeezed itself into a tight hard ball, as I listened to myself.

And I watched Gigi Boudakian's smart, kind face go all watery with pity for me, and for this dead person I was talking about.

But even that wasn't the worst. No, the worst was when I turned back to catch Fran, Fran my hero, my strong and great sister Fran, sitting there getting all busted up and flushed as she looked at me with something like the same pity, and something like fury, too.

"The way you make things look is not the way they really are, Keir," Fran said, leaning forward to try and put a hand on my knee. I pushed her hand away. "You make things up to be what you want them to be. And Ray lets you."

"Shut up, Fran. Don't you say anything bad about Ray."

"I don't want to hurt you, Keir. I love you, and I love Ray, too. But I have to love Ray from a distance. He's not healthy for me. He's not healthy for you."

My mind shot to Ray, to Ray alone, to Ray in the house, to Ray at the Risk table all by himself. I felt my own eyes welling up at the thought of me and my dad playing our yearlong game together, our innocent, ongoing Risk game that wasn't any trouble to anybody. I should have stayed there, I thought. Should never have gotten up from that table across from Ray.

I couldn't speak.

"Ray is not a strong man, Keir," she went on mercilessly. "And we needed him to be, especially you. You need to look at yourself, Keir, and look at life and reality a little more clearly, and Ray has never made you do that. You need to take responsibility for yourself, for the things you do, and not make excuses for yourself. I heard, Keir, about all the stuff this year, all the frat boy antics and destroying statues and everything else and instead of getting excited about having you come up here, I started dreading it. You have grown progressively more spoiled and irresponsible, and I am not purely happy you are coming here. Do you hear me? Do you get the magnitude . . ."

Whether I heard it or got it or whatever, I was never going to be able to tell her. Because I was choking near to death with what was inside. And I was holding back what was already feeling like a full-blown, full-force monsoon of fear and hate and disgust and self-pity.

And then I didn't have to tell her at all.

"That's enough, I think," said Gigi Boudakian. She pulled me by my weak and pathetic hand, right up out of that rank college sofa. "I don't actually know you, Fran, or Mary, but I can tell you that Keir talks about you all the time. And he talks about you like you are angels. And I can tell you that whatever flaws he has—and nobody's going to argue that he hasn't got them—he is a sweet and soft-hearted guy at core. And if he says that your family was once an amazing and beautiful thing and his heart is broken now because it isn't what it was, then I am inclined to believe him.

"This is a good guy, Fran. Innocent he is not. But he is a good guy. Maybe if he does make things up, maybe he made up the part about how wonderful *you* were."

Just there where I would have expected Fran's back to get further up and her approach to get harder, I figured wrong again. Her voice went suddenly all soft.

"I think probably he did," she said.

Nobody had anything to say to that. We stared for a few seconds.

"We shouldn't have come here like this," Gigi said with her good timing and manners, "and I'm sorry for that, Fran. Come on, Keir."

She tugged me the short distance to the door. She didn't even turn back as she opened the door and we went out, and whatever protest Fran might have been making was lost on me because I couldn't even make it out. There was nothing but Gigi.

And I wanted to cry more than ever.

We walked around the campus again. We didn't talk about it, we just did it. It seemed like the best thing to do. Like the only thing to do. There was no limousine, nor would there be one, though Gigi didn't know that yet.

"I'm sorry," she said, putting an arm around me at the hip. It was warm and reassuring the way we bumped off each other as we tried to get into the rhythm of walking together. "It really is terrible when people let you down."

"It is. It's inexcusable," I said. "And I'm sorry too. For Carl letting you down."

"Yes," she said, "Carl."

We didn't walk the whole way around like before, though that would have been my idea of the best plan in the world. We stopped at the mansion houses when the inevitable happened and Gigi inquired about the ride home.

"Shouldn't we get back there?" she said. "When's he coming?"

What was I thinking? That would be a good question. I had actually allowed myself to believe that this moment wouldn't come. So what did I think would come in its place? That's the thing right there, that's the place where I tend to make mistakes. I am good at that, at refusing to accept that something bad is coming when it may seem obvious that something bad is coming. But I'm less good at figuring out what is going to come in its place. Because something always has to come in its place, doesn't it? Something always has to come and fill in that space.

"You want a pill?" I offered generously.

"Quit fooling, Keir," she said, beginning to walk ahead toward the dorms.

When I was behind her, I popped a pill.

"I'm getting really tired now," Gigi Boudakian said in an all-new, all-adorable tired voice.

"Well, that's why," I croaked through a dry, choked throat, "the pill is a good idea."

"The pill is not a good idea," she said. She sounded like she was moving quickly now through the stages of sleepiness. This stage was grouchier. "Let's just go and wait for the car."

Right there. Right there was when I should have admitted what I'd done. It would have been the right thing to do. It would have been the right moment.

"Okay," I said instead.

We sat on the curb in front of my sister's building for over an hour. Gigi Boudakian leaned over and dozed on my shoulder while I sat upright, rigid, wide awake now and buzzy. I was playing along in this fantasy where a limousine was coming any minute, and even though I knew it wasn't coming I was waiting for it—and the kicker was, I was having a pretty all right time of it.

If I could just keep her for a little while. If I could just hold her for a little while. There, glued to my shoulder, she could sleep and I could watch over her and I wouldn't even mind, sitting on the hard curb in front of my cold sister's awful little new home. I could love this.

"Ke-ir," Gigi Boudakian moaned, two syllables, child-sleepy, eyes still shut. "Ke-ir. Where is the car? Why isn't the car here? I am dead. I'm starting to get a headache. I don't feel good."

She had finished my short-lived idyll. The time had come. I couldn't expect to avoid the truth any longer.

"I guess he's not coming," I said. "I guess something went wrong. Maybe he came when we were out walking. I don't know, Gigi. Rollo can be funny."

"Oh, Keir. Keir, what are we going to do? What time is it?"

"It's almost four."

"In the morning?"

"Afraid so."

"Oh, no! We'll have to stay with your sister."

"Absolutely not," I said. "I'll sleep on the street first."

"Well, I won't. What are we going to do?"

I knew what we could do. Don't know why I didn't think of it before. Maybe I did. Maybe part of me did. I knew about it, that's for sure, because I had known about it for months.

"There's a place we can stay," I said.

I took sleepy Gigi Boudakian by the hand, pulled her up, and led her on. The sudden whoosh of blood to my head made me all floaty as we walked and talked.

"There's a building down this way, at the far edge of the campus. In some woods. It's for guests. Visiting family, visiting sports people, speakers, conferences, stuff like that. It's empty most of the time, and definitely at this point in the year."

She looked at me sideways. "What's it got to do with you?"

"I have a key."

"You have a *key*? Who are you? You don't even go to this school yet."

"It's not my key, exactly. It's the football team's key. For their use. For our use. It's in a spot in the rosebush out front. A key to open the front door, and another one for the last room on the top floor. It's one of the perks."

She stopped walking.

"What?" I said. "It's perfectly all right. It's okay."

"Oh, Keir, I don't know. I don't know about this at all."

"What's not to know? We don't have a lot of options. There is nowhere else to go at four in the morning way out here. We'll go up, catch three or four hours sleep, then get the bus back home in the morning. It's the best plan."

She looked at me sideways, but her lids were pulling down again. "I have to sleep," she said.

"I know," I said, walking on, "and we will. We will."

We trudged the rest of the way to the three-floor block at the edge of a wood at the edge of the campus. I got down on my knees and fished out the sandwich bag with the keys, just like the football seniors had shown me. In another minute we were at the top of the industrial staircase and letting ourselves into room 312.

"Honey, we're home," I said.

She looked up at me, exhausted and unamused.

I flipped on the light, a long harsh fluorescent strip down the middle of the ceiling. The room itself was like a jail cell. There were two single beds up against opposing cinder-block walls, and nothing but bare pale linoleum floor between them. In the far corner was an extremely basic oak desk built into the wall and carved with lots of initials and primitive artwork. The place smelled strongly like rubber. Tire rubber. There was a single window on the wall directly opposite the door.

"Please turn that light off," Gigi said as she sat on her bed, the one close to the window. I did, and watched as she dropped first her bag, then her shoes, on the floor. I took off my jacket, threw it at the desk, missed, left it there. I kicked off my shoes and sat there on the side of my bed, staring at nothing.

She was there, like a ghost. I wasn't even aware of any movement before Gigi Boudakian, in angel-blue light, was there in front of me. She bent down, put one hand on my shoulder, and kissed me.

It was a nice kiss. It was nicer than any other kiss she'd ever given me, and it was not a brother kiss. She let it touch just the corner of my mouth, and stay there for three, four seconds, just long enough to burn her brand into my flesh for life. It was nicer than any kiss anyone ever gave me, or ever would.

And then she was done. Her face floated there in front of my face for a few seconds more.

"Remember, first thing, we are out of here," she said in a weary, raspy whisper.

"Uh-huh," I said.

And she was back to bed. I wasn't even lying down yet. I was still sitting there upright, in the space of the kiss. I was still living in it, happily ever after.

"Lie down, Keir," Gigi said kindly.

I tipped over sideways and lay there.

Before minutes had passed, I could hear the soft snuffling noise that must have been the Gigi Boudakian version of a snore. I listened to it, closer, like a lovely old record. I listened to her breathing for a long time. I was a lucky man.

I was not a sleepy man, however, and I knew I would not be for some time. I knew I needed help, and I rooted in my pocket for it. I found the antidote, the reliable come-down friends that Quarterback Ken kept in quantity. I swallowed one. I lay there for a minute and realized the futility. I swallowed the other one.

I felt the tears rolling out of the outside corners of my eyes, along my temples, into my ears. I always hated when that happened, when the tears would run that way because you were on your back looking up when the tears decided to come. Tears in your ears will make you crazy, and they were making me crazy and making more tears come.

I was so lonely. I was so so lonely.

I wasn't up to anything other than not being alone.

"Gigi," I said softly, standing by her bed. "Gigi, can I come over?"

She didn't say anything. She was breathing deeply, peacefully.

"Gigi, I want to come over," I said, and she didn't say yes or no.

I looked over her. The space between Gigi Boudakian and the wall was plenty of space. She was huddled up on the edge of the bed and so there was more than enough room for me. It seemed all right. I thought about it—I didn't *not* think about it, which is a problem sometimes. And it felt all right.

Quietly, easily, I went to the end of the bed and climbed my way up into the space like a cat. Like a pet cat just coming up to get some warmth and not disturbing anybody.

Gigi shifted. She was on her side, facing away, and then she sort of backed into me some. I could smell her hair. It smelled faintly of oil, faintly of smoke. I let my face hover there, in the tangle of Gigi Boudakian's hair on the pillow.

Until she rolled over. She rolled over and all of a sudden there she was, Gigi's face there right up to my face on the pillow. Her long eyelashes looked like they had lengthened in her sleep, and were now tickling her cheekbones. Her skin, with the moon angling in from the window, was polished amber marble.

But her mouth. Gigi Boudakian's sleeping mouth was a living, thriving thing, heart-shaped and full and pushed out in the direction of the world like a gift.

It was all right to kiss her lips. It did not seem all right not to kiss them. I kissed Gigi Boudakian there on her lips, first lightly as if I did not want to be known, then harder and realer like I definitely did.

Her lips were so soft I could have fallen right in. I would have loved to.

But the glory of it was that she kissed me back.

She did not open her eyes at first, but there was a definite shift, from Gigi Boudakian lying there being kissed like Sleeping Beauty, to Beauty waking, to feeling it, to her kissing me. I put my arms around her then, and she kissed me more. Her eyes were still closed, but she made a sound, a sad sound straight out of the heart without any voice, like a moan, a cry, a call like one lost bird to another and I knew what I was doing was right when I recognized that sound as the same lonely sound my own heart was making, my better heart, the exact same sound it was making and had been making for a long time.

I had my clothes off so easy it was like there was a backstage assistant helping me. "I love you, Gigi Boudakian," I said, kissing her eyes, which were still closed. Kissing her mouth.

I did not stop kissing her, not enough to even let us breathe. She was moaning then, moaning that familiar heart sound that I knew, that I wanted, and she was moving, leaning, rolling. Her eyes were open now, and she was moaning, and she was moaning loud, and I was pressing my mouth so hard to hers it hurt, but it was right. It was so right. I held her hands in my hands tightly on the pillow above her head, and I held her, her face, her mouth, her whole being, with mine, holding her as completely as one person can hold another person.

'm worn down. Everything is catching up with me now and I can feel myself physically melting down. She is doing nothing, Gigi Boudakian, other than kneeling there in the middle of the floor in the middle of the tire-smelling room, but she is wearing me down. She won't even sit on the bed or anything, and she won't even listen to what I am saying.

"Do you even know what rape is?" I say to her.

She doesn't respond. She kneels and kneels like some kind of a religious figure, some kind of skinny Buddha or something, and it's as if she is getting stronger somehow while I am getting weaker.

"Okay, nobody is really innocent, are they? In real life. Nobody at all can say exactly that they are innocent. I don't want to prove to you that I'm innocent, Gigi, I just want to prove to you that I'm good. Good is better than innocent, because at least good is *possible.*"

She says nothing.

"Remember, you said I was good? You said, just last night to Fran, you said I was a good guy? That was me. This is still me. That's what you're forgetting."

I am sitting on my bed now, by the door, and the rubber smell is stronger than ever. Like tires spinning out on pavement.

"Do you smell that, that rubber smell? Terrible, isn't it? Where do you suppose it comes from? Look at all those lovely pine trees out there. That's what we should be smelling, don't you think? The pine trees?"

Nothing.

"You haven't even tried, Gigi. At least I am trying to do something. At least I get credit for that."

Nothing.

"You know what it feels like? Okay, Gigi. You know? I'll tell you. It feels like, like I have two hearts. I have two hearts, and they are both working at the same time. And sometimes they are working in the same direction for the same thing and I can move redwood trees out of your way and then plant them again. But more of the time they are working on two different things at the same time and they make an unholy mess. And that's what happens.

"But remember when you said I was a good guy? You should remember that."

I don't get nothing this time. Gigi Boudakian gets up off the floor, stares at me, then takes a seat on the edge of her bed.

"Good guys aren't rapists," she says flatly.

Oh thank God. Finally. For the first time in a lifetime, we are getting through the fog. She is seeing me again, and I am hearing what I should be hearing. She is seeing what she is supposed to see, and I could fall to the floor and kiss her feet.

"That's right," I say, nearly whining with appreciation. "That is what I have been trying to explain to you. It was just, it was just bad connections—"

"And you are a rapist," she adds, flatter still.

I am pulling my hair now. I could scream. I could wilt. There is very little left in me.

"I didn't rape you, Gigi."

Nothing.

I get up, walk over to her bed. I crouch down to her just the way she did to me so sweetly hours before, when she kissed me hours before. The best kiss in anybody's life, just those tiny few hours before.

I stare into her eyes. More to the point, I get her to stare into mine. I am still certain, still lock-certain, that if she could see me for real again, this could all be put right again. I stare.

And I wait.

And I stare.

Cold as crystal, her eyes remain, cold as crystal.

I kiss her. I kiss Gigi Boudakian as softly and as full-heartedly as I know how, and when I do it I love her all over again, more than ever, again.

This is all we need. Gigi Boudakian cannot possibly think the wrong things when she remembers my loving her so. Nobody can be loved as hard as I love her and not be moved by that. She just needs to remember.

I tip her back onto the bed. I start kissing her differently now, harder, with passion, with love, with fury, I pull at her dress, get her shoulder exposed, and I press the full weight and length of my body down over the full length of hers as I swing her legs up onto the bed. I kiss her neck, and her ears, and her eye.

She feels like a long tall rag doll. I jerk back. She hasn't even closed her eye when I kiss it. It is the most chilling, most creeping thing, and I push up off her.

I stare down, and now she is staring into me. She is seeing me now.

I am still spooked, but I lower myself again and am kissing her again, loving her again, and watching her eyes. Her beautiful soft chocolate Gigi Boudakian eyes, frozen in place on me. In me.

And I stop.

We are there, for an eternity, my body still moving slightly like an insect with its head yanked off. I can feel horror lines grooving my face.

I am horrified. I am sick.

I pull away, jump up. I back away from her, all the way across the room from her, and she doesn't so much as blink. I fall back onto my bed, let myself fall, let myself go flat and lifeless. I turn over on my side, looking in her direction, and I curl into a tighter and tighter coil.

After a very short pause, Gigi Boudakian stands. She gathers herself, gathers her things, fixes her dress, her pretty, pretty dress from pretty yesterday. She has her shoes in her hand and her bag on her arm as she moves, with unfathomable grace, past me and out the door.

I roll over onto my other side, face the cinder-block wall, and wait for whoever is going to come for me.

ABOUT THE AUTHOR

Chris Lynch is the Printz Honor–winning author of *Freewill* and other highly acclaimed young adult novels, including *Gold Dust, Iceman, Gypsy Davey,* and *Shadow Boxer,* all ALA Best Books for Young Adults. He is also the author of *Elvin Extreme, Whitechurch,* and *All the Old Haunts.* Lynch holds an MA from the writing program at Emerson College. He lives in Scotland, and he continues to work on new literary projects.

Exciting fiction from three-time Newbery Honor author
GARY PAULSEN

Aladdin Paperbacks and Simon Pulse
Simon & Schuster Children's Publishing
www.SimonSays.com

UGLIES
SCOTT WESTERFELD

Everybody gets to be supermodel gorgeous. What could be wrong with that?

In this futuristic world, all children are born "uglies," or freaks. But on their sixteenth birthdays they are given extreme makeovers and turned "pretty." Then their whole lives change. . .

PRAISE FOR *UGLIES*:

★ "An exciting series. . . . The awesome ending thrills with potential." —*Kirkus Reviews*

★ "Ingenious . . . high-concept YA fiction that has wide appeal." —*Booklist*

★ "Highly readable with a convincing plot that incorporates futuristic technologies and a disturbing commentary on our current public policies. Fortunately, the cliff-hanger ending promises a sequel." —*School Library Journal*

PUBLISHED BY SIMON PULSE